He stepped awa
her with purpo

She could hardly bre
and pulled her into h
her body, not allowing her feet to touch the ground.

"I thought you'd never get here," he whispered into her hair. "If I don't kiss you right here and now, I'm not going to make it."

"I want you to kiss me," she confessed, inching her lips over his smooth, shaven jaw to the compelling mouth she'd longed to taste. Ally wanted him in such an elemental way, there was no thought of her holding back. His hunger matched hers as their mouths met in a fiery explosion of need she had no way of controlling.

Ally hadn't known a man's embrace for several years, but nothing had prepared her for the kiss of her Texas Ranger except in her dreams. But this was no dream, and Luckey was taking her to a place she'd never been before.

Dear Reader,

I've always had a love for languages. At my school, a priest from the cathedral came to my junior high to teach us Latin. I LOVED Latin. It helped me understand English in a wonderful way and taught me how to speak correctly. I can still remember the nominative, genitive, accusative, dative and ablative cases that told me whether to say I or me, or he or him. Marvelous!

Then I traveled to Switzerland and learned to speak French. What a joy! My Latin helped me make sense of the diplomatic language of the world. I took Spanish and always wanted to study Italian. My sister lived in Perugia, Italy, and speaks beautiful Italian. My daughter studied in Siena, Italy, and her Italian is wonderful. I've been very envious of both of them.

Last year I found out about an old secret language learned by a few elite women in China. I won't tell you any more than that. You'll have to read *Her Texas Ranger Hero* to know why it fascinated me so much. I knew I had to write a novel where that language featured heavily in the plot and brought the hero and heroine together.

Enjoy!

Rebecca Winters

HER TEXAS RANGER HERO

REBECCA WINTERS

HARLEQUIN® WESTERN ROMANCE®

Recycling programs
for this product may
not exist in your area.

ISBN-13: 978-0-373-75727-5

Her Texas Ranger Hero

Copyright © 2016 by Rebecca Winters

This edition published by arrangement with Harlequin Books S.A.

For questions and comments about the quality of this book, please contact us at CustomerService@Harlequin.com.

® and TM are trademarks of Harlequin Enterprises Limited or its corporate affiliates. Trademarks indicated with ® are registered in the United States Patent and Trademark Office, the Canadian Intellectual Property Office and in other countries.

Printed in U.S.A.

Rebecca Winters, whose family of four children has now swelled to include five beautiful grandchildren, lives in Salt Lake City, Utah, in the land of the Rocky Mountains. With canyons and high alpine meadows full of wildflowers, she never runs out of places to explore. They, plus her favorite vacation spots in Europe, often end up as backgrounds for her romance novels, because writing is her passion, along with her family and church.

Rebecca loves to hear from readers. If you wish to email her, please visit her website, cleanromances.com.

Books by Rebecca Winters

Harlequin American Romance

Lone Star Lawmen

The Texas Ranger's Bride
The Texas Ranger's Nanny
The Texas Ranger's Family

Hitting Rocks Cowboys

In a Cowboy's Arms
A Cowboy's Heart
The New Cowboy
A Montana Cowboy

Daddy Dude Ranch

The Wyoming Cowboy
Home to Wyoming
Her Wyoming Hero

Chapter One

"Yoo-hoo—I'm back! Does anyone care?"

Ally's mother beat her to the front door of the ranch house, where her father had just walked in. His black hair with its streaks of silver made him distinguished looking. He put his briefcase on the floor and the three of them hugged.

"I decided to fly all night from Washington, DC, so I could surprise you. You're both a glorious sight!" After kissing her mom, he turned to kiss Ally's cheek.

"I'm so glad you're home." She kissed him back. "I was just about to leave for work, but I'll be home later and we'll celebrate."

"Wait—I have a present for you." He reached down and opened the case to pull out a letter. "I believe you've been waiting for this. It came in my diplomatic pouch yesterday."

"Soo-Lin!"

"Who else?"

"I haven't had a letter from her in two months!" Soo-Lin was one of Ally's best friends. She couldn't wait to hear all her news. Since Ally's family had returned from China last summer, she'd hungered for Soo-Lin's periodic letters. "I'll take this with me." She hugged them both again. "I'll be back soon to help you, Mom."

"All right, darling."

Ally knew her parents would appreciate some quiet time together, and flew out the door to her car. She wanted to open the letter right away, but would have to put off reading it until she reached her office.

Twenty minutes later she pulled into the faculty parking lot of the University of Texas at Austin campus. "Hi, Nedra," she said to the receptionist as she hurried in. "Have any students been by asking for me?"

"Not yet."

"That's good. I'm running late." She made her way down the hall. After unlocking the door, she rushed inside and settled in before pulling the letter out of her purse.

Dear Friend, Thank you for your last letter. I can't get used to you being so far away now. I'm not happy about it, but if you are happy, then that is good. You asked what happened when I went to the doctor. She said my fallopian tubes are blocked and suggests we try in vitro fertilization if we want children.

Oh, no…

My husband has been quiet about it, but that is Zheng's way. Nine years and still no baby.

Now we know why. I wouldn't blame him if he wanted to leave me.

Ally cringed to hear those words. IVF was a very viable option for Soo-Lin, but Ally needed to give her a pep talk in person.

Mother is well enough. Father is doing poorly. His heart is not good, but the jewelry business has never been better and Zheng has been over-seeing the other showrooms to ease the load. He has a fine business mind, like my father, and they see many things the same.

Soo-Lin's parents were wonderful. So was Zheng. Ally loved them all.

What I have to tell you next is very upsetting to me and has devastated our family.

Ally couldn't imagine. Her heart rate sped up.

Maybe you don't remember my third cousin Yi. He came to my wedding with his wife and two children. But something awful has hap-pened. Three weeks ago their sixteen-year-old daughter, Yu Tan, didn't come home from school. One of her friends said she ran off with a man from a disco club in the city where she often went dancing without permission. I don't believe it. Yu Tan is a sweet, well-brought-up young woman with plans to make the Olympic team and go to college. She's won all kinds of awards in gymnastics.

Ally did remember her, but hadn't seen her since the wedding. Yu-Tan would have been around seven at the time.

I know she wouldn't go off with a man like that. I don't trust that her friend is telling the truth. Now a tragedy has happened, because my cousin has disowned her, his own daughter! He listens to his father, who is the head of their family and a very forbidding man. You know what I mean. He believes in the old traditions and closes his mind to reason.

Both my cousin and his father believe she has disgraced the entire Tan family. My mother does not agree and says the grandfather's pride is too great to help find his own granddaughter. I've begged my father to talk to him, but he says it will do no good. He will not listen. This isn't right, Ally.

No. Nothing about it sounded right. Soo-Lin belonged to an upper-class family that didn't tolerate embarrassment. Ally could feel her friend's pain.

I've given you enough bad news for now. Write me back as soon as you can. You'll always be my best friend. Soo-Lin.

When Ally got home, she'd write a letter and ask her father to send it with his classified correspondence. As she was putting the letter back in her purse, one of her students walked into the office. It was time to get to work.

RANGER JAMES DAVIS had just arrived at Texas Rangers' headquarters in downtown Austin when his cell phone rang. He clicked on. "Davis here."

"Luckey?"

Only family and close friends called him by his nickname. "Hey, Randy."

"Do you have time to talk?"

"I always have time for my little bro." Though he had a Monday morning meeting scheduled with his boss, TJ, he could spare a few minutes. TJ was the captain of the Austin-based Company H, where Luckey had been assigned since becoming a Ranger. "What's going on? How are Lisa and the two cutest little girls in Texas?"

"We're all great and wish you'd drop by more often."

Luckey swung by the makeshift lunchroom located on the second floor of the building for a cup of coffee and a doughnut. Taking a bite, he entered his own office and sank down in his chair. "Sorry it's been so long. My last undercover case was no picnic and took forever to solve."

"So I heard. Dad said three escaped felons are in the federal slammer because of you. Guys are singing your praises all over the department." Luckey smiled. Their dad had recently retired as sheriff for Travis County and was now doing full-time ranching, but he'd never be out of the loop. "You're becoming a bigger legend than our original Texas Ranger ancestor," his brother added.

"Knock it off, Randy. Still enjoying your work as a mounted police officer?"

"It's getting old. At least I was put on the day shift three days ago."

Luckey frowned. "I thought you liked it."

"The horse part I love, but more and more I know I want to be a Ranger."

He'd heard that from his brother several times before and took another sip of his coffee. "That means a lot more hours away from the fam. I don't have a wife and children, so that isn't a problem for me." Never again. "How does Robin feel about it?"

"She said that if it's what I want, I should do it."

"You married a terrific woman."

Luckey's ex-wife had felt the exact opposite. She couldn't handle his work as a Ranger and acted on it by divorcing him and moving to Houston. But that was old news.

Randy's voice lowered. "I didn't mean to remind you of the past."

"I know you didn't." Luckey had the greatest brother in the world. He was thirty to Luckey's thirty-two. "If that's your goal, I'm behind you."

"It's all I've been able to think about for the last year. Remember that body my partner and I found dumped on the street on our beat last week? It's the fourth one in the last ten months. Though each was discovered in a different area, I believe they're all related. But the detective who arrived on the scene disagrees."

Luckey was listening intently to his brother, who was no fool. He remembered clips on the news, but hadn't paid much attention. "What do your instincts tell you?" This was Randy's case, but Luckey was always interested.

"All four bodies have been young Chinese and Indonesian women, which smells like human trafficking to me. When I pointed this out to him, he said he wasn't ready to make an assumption like that quite yet. He said coincidence could play a role, or some copycat criminals who heard the news on the media could've decided to pull the same stunts for the sheer pleasure of creating chaos."

At a trafficking conference Luckey had recently attended, he'd learned that although Asians represented only 6 percent of Austin's 800,000 residents, their population had surged by 60 percent since 2000. It was the fastest-growing group in the city by percentage and tripled the rate of Austin's overall growth.

"It doesn't sound like a coincidence to me," Luckey concurred. "Have you discussed this with anyone else?"

"Nope. You know I can't."

"Listen—I want to talk to you some more about this, but I've got to go in to a meeting right now. This one will probably last an hour. Expect a call from me after I get out."

"Thanks."

Luckey clicked off and headed for TJ's office at the end of the hall. The gray-haired captain nodded as he walked in. "I'm surprised to see you remembered. I thought you might be home enjoying some well-deserved sleep after your last case."

"Not me. I like work."

His boss nodded again. "I know you do. But one of these days you need to take some time off."

"I do better being busy."

TJ's eyes filled with concern. "I don't want you to burn out."

Luckey blinked. "You think I am?"

"Of course not. But my famous Four Sons of the Original Forty Texas Rangers have done a hell of a job for the department this last year. I want you to know you can have the time off if you feel you need it."

"Can I take a rain check on that?"

He nodded.

Good. "So what smorgasbord of corruption and evil are you going to lay out for me this morning?"

TJ chuckled. "Take your pick of the latest Most Wanted cases that have come across my desk." He riffled through the pile of files in front of him. "Armed robbery and murder of an armored-car guard. Kidnapping and brutal murder of two women, one of whom was set on fire in her wheelchair. The murder of a prominent CEO...or this latest one—a dead body dumped on the streets, a case that has the police detective stumped."

"I'll take that one," Luckey said without hesitation.

TJ handed him the file. "Of course, it's not a co-incidence that your brother is mentioned in the abstract."

"Nothing gets past you, Captain."

His boss made an odd sound. "Go ahead and read it. Afterward I'll tell you what the police commissioner told me."

Luckey read the short paragraph to himself. "March 2. 2:20 a.m. Officers Mendez and Davis came across one Asian female of undetermined age found dead a block from the Underground Nightclub in the warehouse district of Austin, Texas. No witnesses. Died of gunshot wound to the back."

"It's sparse, all right," he finally muttered.

TJ leaned forward. "The commissioner informed me that this is the fourth unsolved dumped body in less than a year. One was Indonesian, the other three of Chinese ethnicity. None had ties to friends or family found so far. No matches of their pictures to passport photos from China or Indonesia. No evidence that these girls were in school here, or had jobs and were here on working visas.

"The police have circulated pictures of the women everywhere, hoping someone will identify them, but investigations haven't turned up anything."

Luckey frowned. "Did they cover the strip clubs and spas, not to mention the massage parlors?" To be thorough they needed to check out modeling studios, cantinas and residential brothels as well, but it was a grueling process.

"If they did, they've had no success."

Luckey had his work cut out for him. "Sex trafficking is also common in the agricultural, restaurant and nail salon industries."

TJ shot him a glance. "The commissioner is convinced they were victims of trafficking and has turned the case over to us. What does your brother think? Between him and your father, you're not all Davises for nothing."

The compliment didn't escape Luckey. "Randy disagrees that the deaths were random acts of violence. He sees a pattern and believes they're related."

"I'm sure he's right. If anyone can figure it out, you can. Where are you going to start?"

"I want to see the latest body."

"If you need backup later, just holler. Good luck."

"Thanks, Captain."

Intrigued by this new case, Luckey got up from the chair and headed out of the building to the car park. Once inside his XC90 Volvo, he drove to the county coroner's office. En route he phoned his brother.

"Guess what? The case of the dead body you discovered has been turned over to the Rangers by the police commissioner."

"What?"

"I was surprised, too. The captain agrees with your assessment that the four deaths are related. I've taken the case. Kind of gives you chills." When Randy's application to join the Rangers came up, Luckey would remind his boss of their conversation.

"Well, what do you know? I'd give anything to be working this case with you."

"As long as we keep it to ourselves, who says you can't help when you're off duty? We've done it before. I'm going to the morgue to find out as much as I can. I'll get back to you."

"Thanks."

TEN MINUTES LATER, Luckey knocked on the door of the coroner's private office.

"Luckey? What can I do for you?"

"How are you, Dr. Wolff?" He'd had a working relationship with the forensics expert for years. Luckey handed him the file.

The older man studied it before nodding. "I examined the body last week. She was probably a sixteen- or seventeen-year-old Chinese woman, shot in the back with a .357 cal SIG Sauer."

"How long had she been dead when she was found?"

"Six or seven hours."

"According to my source, three other bodies of Asian women have been found on the streets in the last ten months and there've been no arrests made. I'd like to know their approximate ages, manner of death, everything you've got."

"You're welcome to the information in the files. But first, come over here. There's something unique about this particular body. I would like to show you a piece of evidence that has me puzzled."

Dr. Wolff walked to a shelf holding some labeled

boxes and took one down. After lifting the lid, he showed Luckey the soiled, bloodstained, pale pink silk dress inside, folded so that the hole made by a bullet was visible.

"The young woman was wearing this when her body was brought in. Here. Put on some gloves."

Luckey pulled out a pair from the carton and slipped them on.

"Go ahead and look on the underside of the skirt," the doctor urged.

Curious, he turned it inside out. To his surprise he saw writing on the material, all the way around from the waist down, unusual characters that meant nothing to him. His brows knit together. "Is this Chinese?"

"It looks like a form of it, but none of our experts here recognize it. Don't let your eyes deceive you. What is written here was not done in red ink, but blood. *Her* blood."

Luckey moaned inwardly. "I need copies of the pictures you took of the writing."

"Certainly. Anything you want."

"Did the detective investigating this case know about this?"

"He examined the inscriptions, but as I said, we couldn't tell him anything about them. I have no idea if he's following up on any of it."

"Can I see the body now?"

"Right this way."

Luckey was taken to the morgue and shown the deceased. She'd been a lovely young woman with refined features and long black hair. He returned to the coroner's office and gathered information from the files of the four bodies, photocopying everything for his own records. The reports revealed three of the deceased were of Chinese origin and one was Indonesian, as he'd been told. They were all short—between five-one and five-two—and most likely sixteen or seventeen years old.

"The clothing is different on each one," he muttered thoughtfully.

The doctor nodded. "I performed the autopsies. The Indonesian victim was strangled. Hers was the first body found. The second victim was stabbed in the chest. The third girl was wearing only a slip, had bloodshot eyes and died from suffocation. As you know, this latest one was shot in the back.

"These women appear to have been innocent victims. They were attacked and murdered before being transported to another spot to be dumped. But this latest victim was different from the others. She had broad shoulders and powerfully muscular legs. This suggests that she was into sports—or perhaps she was a ballet dancer or gymnast.

"And there's something else you'll see in the forensics report. I found a substance on the sleeves of her dress. Whoever dragged her body had DMSO cream on his or her hands."

"What's that, exactly?" Luckey asked.

"Some kind of topical painkiller."

"You didn't find traces of it on the other three bodies?"

"No."

"Details like that are going to help me build this case," he murmured as he examined the writing on the fabric again. "I've never seen anything so strange before. Did you find out if there was something special about this dress?"

"It's silk, well made. There's no label to tell us where it might have been bought or what manufacturer made it."

After thanking Dr. Wolff, Luckey tossed his gloves, picked up the files and photocopies and drove back to headquarters. He was happy to find his boss still in his office. Luckey knocked on the door and was told to come in. He put the information from Dr. Wolff on TJ's desk.

"Take a look at all this. What we've got here is evidence that these four young Asians were violently murdered. When you asked me to attend that trafficking conference a month ago, I was impressed by the panel. It included everyone from Homeland Security, Immigration and Customs Enforcement, the US Postal Inspection and the US Attorney General for the eastern US.

"The deaths of these four women fall in line with the latest statistics from the National Human Trafficking Hotline. To date, it has received more calls from Texas than any other state in the union."

"That makes sense, considering our extremely diverse population," TJ mused.

Luckey nodded. "Our close proximity to Mexico makes this the most crossed international border. But I never realized that Texas contains a quarter of all

American trafficking victims, and that almost a third of the calls to the hotline come from our state."

"That many?"

"I know. I was surprised, too. Twenty percent of the 50,000 people annually trafficked from foreign countries into the United States come through Texas."

TJ shook his head.

"Unfortunately, we haven't yet pinpointed the source of the female trafficking activity coming out of China. But today the coroner showed me two things that might have given us our first lead." Luckey explained about the cream and then he got to the writing. "Check this out."

He opened the file and showed his boss pictures of the mysterious characters written in blood on the underside of the latest victim's dress. "I'm not sure what this means, but it could open up this case once I get some answers. No one in forensics can read it or translate it. I'm thinking I need to find an expert in Chinese as a place to start. I'll call the language department at the UT Austin and go from there."

"Excellent start, Luckey. Keep me posted."

ALLY DUNCAN CHECKED her watch. Ten after three in the afternoon. Her graduate students had turned in their theses. Now that it was spring break, she could spend her time studying them before setting up appointments for her students to come in and defend them, once classes started again.

She texted her mom that she'd be home in half an hour. They were planning to take some of the orphans to Zilker Park. Years earlier, Ally's father had established the Austin orphanage for Chinese children with disabilities. They would ride the Zilker Zephyr miniature train and enjoy a picnic on the grounds before dark. With her father back from Washington, maybe he'd go with them.

After reaching for her handbag in the desk drawer, Ally started for the door and opened it, only to collide with a tall, rock-hard, masculine body. "I'm sorry," the man murmured, and grasped her upper arms to steady her, while securing a file folder under his arm.

After noting the badge on the pocket of his khaki shirt identifying him as a Texas Ranger, she lifted her head and let out a quiet gasp. The man was gorgeous. He had neatly trimmed dark blond hair and rugged features, but it was his brown eyes roving appreciatively over her face that infused her with warmth. She stepped back, forcing him to release her.

"I was looking for Dr. Duncan." His deep voice resonated in the room. "I'm James Davis with the Texas Rangers."

She swallowed hard, unable to remember the last time she'd met anyone so attractive. "You've found her. I was just leaving, obviously, but it's apparent you're here on official business."

"*You're* the Director of Asian Studies?" he blurted.

Ally took a quick breath. "I'm not what you expected?"

The hard line of his compelling mouth softened into a smile. "Frankly, no."

She chuckled. "You don't fit the type of student I

normally see in my classes, either. Please, come in and sit down."

He waited until she'd gone back to her chair behind the desk. "The secretary out front said that spring break has started and I might not find you in, but I took a chance, anyway."

Ally's cheeks were burning; she could feel it. She cursed herself for acting like a starstruck teenager instead of a twenty-eight-year-old woman meeting her first legendary Texas Ranger. "How can I help you?" she asked.

"First, may I ask you a question? Has anyone from the police department been here to talk to you yet?"

She looked surprised. "No. No one."

He removed the file from under his arm and opened it to retrieve some pages, which he handed to her. "I'm just starting an investigation. These photos were taken by a forensics expert after the latest body of a young Chinese girl was brought into the morgue last week."

Latest?

Just like that the conversation had turned to something hideous, something Ally was very familiar with. Women from the Hunan Province of China were noted for their beauty. Men from all over the world were willing to pay exorbitant amounts of money to traffickers in order to enslave these poor young women. It was too sad and ghastly to dwell on. Her hands trembled a little as she lifted the first page and stared at the photocopy.

"Do you recognize this?"

Nothing could have surprised her more when she saw that the page contained writing rather than a woman's picture. *Not just any writing, though.* The realization of what she was looking at caused Ally to break out in a cold sweat. Reading it, she felt her stomach muscles clench. She lifted the next page and the next, until she'd read the horrifying contents of all six, then she shot to her feet.

"Where did you come across this?"

"On the victim's body. All this was done in her own blood on the underside of the dress she was wearing."

Ally moaned.

"It's apparent this writing has great significance for you."

She closed her eyes for a moment before she sat back down. "This girl knew she was going to die. The writing is a desperate plea for help in the only way she could communicate in order to prevent her captors from knowing what she was doing."

The Ranger seemed perplexed. "Is it in Chinese, then? The chief forensics expert said they couldn't identify it as such."

Ally took a deep breath before launching into an explanation of what he'd brought her. "This message has been written in Nüshu, a secret language that has evolved over a thousand years in the Hunan Province of China. Nüshu means 'women's language' and comes from a remote area of Yongzhou City in Jiangyong County."

"Why secret?"

"Since the traditional Chinese culture was male-centered, girls were forbidden from any kind of formal education. Nüshu was developed for the women to educate themselves. They were sequestered away from men, and males never learned their language. These sworn sisters took an oath never to reveal their secret language to anyone." Ally picked up the first sheet and studied it again. "This victim was begging for help."

The Ranger studied her intensely. "How do you know all this?"

"For one thing, my best friend, Soo-Lin, was born in Yongzhou and has lived there all her life, except to attend the university in Changsha."

He cocked his attractive blond head. "Which means you've lived there, too?"

Ally sat back in her chair. "I'll have to give you some background. My birth name is Allyson Forrester Duncan."

The moment she said her full name, she saw a flicker of understanding in his eyes. "Duncan…as in former Senator Lawrence Duncan from Austin, then ambassador to China, who now resides here in Austin instead of Washington, DC? It's been in the news."

"He's my father."

"Incredible that you would be the expert I sought out first," he murmured.

"My mother's name is Beatrice Forrester Duncan."

"Forrester," he said aloud. "Her name came up among a few others at a conference I attended recently. The panel praised her work devoted to ending the trafficking of female victims from the Far East here in Texas." He sat forward. "Your mother..."

"Yes. I have fabulous parents and am extremely proud of them."

"How could you not be? Tell me more about your life in China."

"We spent equal time in Beijing and Changsha, for fifteen years. Twice annually we flew home to Austin for two weeks, then went back. Being thirteen years old when we moved, I had tutors and was at the perfect age to pick up Mandarin and Xiang— a dialect of the Changsha region. As soon as I was old enough, I studied at the University of Changsha, under some brilliant teachers.

"Soo-Lin was also studying there and became my close friend. I spent time at her home in Yongzhou and came to love her family, as well. I loved it in China. I never wanted to come home and almost didn't."

"Why did you, then?"

The Ranger was direct, but then, that was his job.

"Last year my father was recalled to Washington. A new ambassador was named, but my dad now serves as a consultant to the president for Far Eastern affairs. So we returned to the Duncan family ranch here in Austin. I joined the university faculty last fall.

"Dad flies back and forth, but my mother and I stay here. She's more involved than ever in her work against trafficking and I help her when I can. We're committed as a family. If I'd stayed in China, I would have missed my parents too terribly."

Ally heard Ranger Davis clear his throat. "You've led a fascinating life. I'm so glad I decided to seek your department out first."

"I must admit the hairs stood up on the back of my neck when I read what's on those pages."

"Mine, too, when you said what they contain."

"It was through Soo-Lin I learned about the secret language."

The Ranger got to his feet. "When we bumped into each other at the door, you said you were on your way out, so I won't keep you. What's your schedule like tomorrow? I'd like to meet again. Get from you an exact translation of what's written on the dress so I can build my case. Out of four similar cases in the last ten months, this is the first piece of tangible evidence to turn up."

"You mean the other bodies were all young Chinese women, too?"

"No. One was Indonesian, but I highly suspect they were all victims of human trafficking. It's imperative we find the person or persons who did this. Unfortunately, there are thousands of trafficking victims currently working in the underground sex trade here in Texas. Trying to escape often means death. Even if these girls don't die, it's nearly impossible for them to get their lives back on track after going through something like this. The men who are responsible need to be caught and locked away forever."

The emotion in his voice convinced Ally that this Ranger was the one who could do it. "I couldn't agree more. Since I don't have a busy schedule right now, why don't you tell me when and where you want to meet?"

"If morning is all right with you, how about we say nine o'clock at the Magnolia Café?"

"Morning is fine," she said. "I realize you're anxious to get going on this case. The Magnolia Café is in my neck of the woods. I suspect you love their chocolate-chip pancakes."

One corner of his mouth lifted.

"So do I," she said, smiling.

He gathered the photocopies and put them back in his folder. "If you're ready, I'll walk you out."

Be still, my heart.

Ally locked her office door behind her and left the building for the faculty parking lot. Several students were milling about outside and one of the young women called out to her. Ally waved, but the other woman was staring so hard at the Ranger, Ally felt a ridiculous sense of pride over the fact that he was escorting her to her car.

She pressed the remote to unlock the door of her silver Audi. "Thank you. I'll see you in the morning."

"Let me get your cell phone number. That way, in case an emergency arises, I'll be able to reach you."

Ally told him her number. After he'd typed it into his phone, his eyes fused with hers, melting her insides. "I'm looking forward to tomorrow. Please remember that for the time being I must ask you to keep this to yourself. If you were to say anything to anyone, even your parents, they could give something away without meaning to that could jeopardize the case. It's for their protection, too."

"I understand."

"I'm sure you do. What should I call you, by the way?"

"Just Ally."

"Until tomorrow, then, Just Ally."

She laughed and watched him head toward the public parking area, then got into her car and pressed her head against the steering wheel. She hated that she'd scanned his left hand for a wedding ring, and hated it even more that the fact that he wasn't wearing one made her so happy.

Had she gone out of her mind? It didn't mean he didn't have a girlfriend. Ally felt shaky after colliding with him in the doorway of her office. Her world had suddenly changed. Fear and excitement waged a war inside her as she pulled out of the parking lot and drove off toward the ranch.

Chapter Two

As soon as Luckey got home, he went straight to the kitchen for a cold cola and ended up in his den. The first thing he did was phone Stan at headquarters. Stan was one of the best forensics experts in the country.

"Luckey? What do you need?"

"What can you tell me about a cream called DMSO?"

"That old underground home remedy?"

"Is that what it is? Traces of it were found on the sleeves of the dress of a suspected murder victim, a sixteen- or seventeen-year-old Chinese girl."

"Hmm. Dimethyl sulfoxide is a by-product of the wood industry, used as a solvent. It acts like a non-steroidal anti-inflammatory. In the 1970s, rumors spread that athletes were using it to cut down on joint pain. The controversy stemmed from the fact that some people believed it to be poisonous, but in reality, DMSO isn't dangerous unless it's injected in gross amounts. Most athletes have since moved on to other treatments."

Luckey made notes. "So the person who dumped the deceased's body in the street had to have been using it at the time. I'm faxing you a report from Dr. Wolff. I need your team to do a global search on DMSO and find a cream that matches the properties on the evidence he identified. Then I can track down where it's sold."

"Will do."

"Thanks."

Once he'd sent the fax, Luckey sat back in his comfortable leather chair and pulled out the six pages of secret writing. To think Ally Duncan had taken one look at these and made sense of them…

What were the odds of him quickly finding anyone else who had her incredible knowledge? All the years he'd been a Ranger, she'd been growing up in an entirely different culture. What an amazing woman.

A gorgeous woman with raven-black hair tumbling to her shoulders and eyes the color of Texas bluebonnets.

When she'd opened her office door, he'd been knocked sideways in more ways than one. The contact had awakened something inside him. She was well-endowed and probably about five foot seven. The scent of her skin and hair, the breathless way she'd responded to him had made Luckey conscious of her as a living, breathing woman.

It had been eight years since his divorce. Since then he'd had relationships with other women, but none had lasted long. He'd always made it clear to the woman he was dating at the time that he wasn't interested in a permanent commitment. Too much damage had been done for him to feel the emotions necessary for a relationship to flourish. But all that changed today. Today he'd been caught totally off guard by a rush of desire so foreign to him he was stunned.

He knew his family worried that he might stay single for good. Luckey hadn't given it a lot of thought until now. *Damn* if meeting Ms. Duncan hadn't pierced through the armor he'd built up around him to the part that had either been asleep or in a deep freeze. What if he still felt this way tomorrow after meeting with her?

Luckey didn't want to experience these feelings again. He couldn't take it. He was just going to meet her for breakfast and record the translation, then he'd get on with the investigation, and that would be the end of it.

Needing to get his mind off Ally ASAP, he phoned Randy. His brother was still on patrol, however, so Luckey left a message that he'd get in touch tomorrow. He thought about calling one of his best friends, but all three were Rangers and he knew they'd be busy working other cases. Restless, he fixed himself a TV dinner, then walked out to the barn and saddled his horse, Persey, who needed the exercise. A good ride would help Luckey put his feelings in perspective.

When it was dark, he came back in and turned on the TV. But he was unable to concentrate on anything. In the end, he returned to the den and pored over the information he'd gathered at the coroner's office. Luckey worked until he couldn't keep his eyes open anymore and then he went to bed.

TUESDAY MORNING HE woke up early to shower and shave. After dressing in a long-sleeved Western shirt and trousers, he went out to feed his horse and noticed he needed to buy more food for him. Once back in the house he remembered that his cleaning lady, Ruth, would be coming by later. She came twice a month and did odd jobs for him. Luckey left her a note to drop by the feed store as well as the grocery store for supplies, and then he took off for the Magnolia Café.

He always felt a certain excitement when he began a new case, but driving to meet with Ally, he recognized an eagerness that had nothing to do with his work.

His pulse picked up speed when he spotted her Audi in the parking lot among at least a dozen cars with license plates from other states. The place got a ton of tourists because the food was reputed to be so good.

He walked in and was greeted by a hostess. "Your party is already at your table," she told him. "She's over in the south corner."

Luckey was surprised. "How did you know?"

The woman smiled. "You're the man with the badge. Can't miss you."

"Thanks," he said.

Ally Duncan stood out from every other female in the room. This morning she'd tied her glossy black hair back at her nape with a simple leather cord.

Those purple-blue eyes fringed by thick black lashes met his as he approached the table. Everything about her was classy. Her nails were manicured in a soft pink shade that matched her lipstick.

"Hi." She smiled at him.

He sat in the chair opposite her and took in the creamy blouse she wore, covered by a sleeveless crochet vest in the same color shot with gold. "Hi, yourself. You were smart to get here early. This place is hopping." He would have suggested a quieter spot, such as a park, for their meeting, but felt a public space would make her more comfortable.

"I remember the last time I came here, with friends. We had to wait an hour to get a table. Since I knew you were in a hurry to get going on this case, I thought I'd make sure we beat the rush."

"Well, I thank you for your consideration."

The waitress came to the table and poured them coffee. Ally murmured, "Go ahead and give her our orders, since you already know what I want."

He smiled. "Chocolate-chip pancakes?"

She smiled back. "Of course."

"Would you like some juice?"

"Sure," she said. "I'll take apple."

"Anything else?"

Ally shook her head.

"Two orders of chocolate-chip pancakes, one apple juice and one glass of OJ, please," he told their waitress.

Once she had left, Luckey was free to focus on the beautiful woman sitting across from him. She wasn't

wearing a ring. How could she still be single? If she
was, it had to be by choice. Had she been wounded
in the past, like he had? Was she reluctant to open up
her heart for fear of being burned again? The question
hung in the air. Of course, she could be in a relationship right now. Either way, he would get an answer
soon, so help him.

She sipped her coffee. "If you'll show me those
papers, I'll look over the writing and translate it for
you once we've eaten."

With those words he was reminded of the reason
they were there. What she said made perfect sense,
but his mind had been on her instead of the case.
"Why don't we eat first, then I'll let you read from
the file while I record you. It will probably be more
horrifying on a second reading."

Quiet reigned as they both drank their coffee.
When she lifted her head, he saw the pained expression that had snuffed the light from her eyes.

He put down his mug. "*Will* it be too horrifying,
second time through?"

"Horrifying and heartbreaking, Ranger Davis."

"Call me Luckey. With an *e*."

Ally cocked her head. "I thought your name was
James."

She remembered. That was something. "Luckey
is my nickname."

"Because you're such a successful Ranger?"

He shook his head. "That's a nice lie, but no, I
inherited it when my parents named me for our ancestor. Luckey Davis was one of the original forty

Rangers serving under Jack Hayes at the Battle of Bandera Pass. That name determined my destiny by osmosis."

"Osmosis instead of genetics? I don't think so. You're the real deal." She chuckled as the waitress came to the table with their food. "Shall we eat?"

They both tucked into their chocolate-chip pancakes. He darted her a glance. "I bet you didn't eat these in China."

"You're right. We had several native cooks who taught me how to prepare local meals from scratch."

"So if there's a revolution—"

"Yikes!" she interjected, causing him to chuckle.

"—and you're not needed as a professor," he continued, "you could open a Chinese restaurant."

"A mediocre one to be sure."

"Ally Duncan? I can say in all honesty that there's nothing mediocre about you."

If he wasn't mistaken, he detected a slight flush on her high cheekbones. But she drawled, "Well, Luckey Davis, it seems we're quite an amazing pair."

He broke into laughter, but doubted anyone noticed, because the room was filled with noise. Though they'd met on a serious matter, she didn't take herself seriously. He liked that about her.

"How would you feel if we went out to your car so you can translate for me?" They'd finished eating. "We're going to need the quiet."

"That's a good idea," she said. He helped her up from the chair and, after he paid the tab, let her walk ahead of him as they made their way to her vehicle.

He had to admit she looked terrific in her designer jeans.

Concentrate on the job, Davis. What he'd have given to have met Ally under other circumstances. He wanted to know if she was involved with another man. And after that he wanted to make plans to see her again that had nothing to do with business. But there were rules a Ranger had to follow. Luckey wanted and needed her trust while he worked on this case. Rules had to come first.

Once they were inside her car, he passed her the papers from the file and pulled out his handheld digital recorder.

Her gaze met his. "Luckey? Before we start, I want to thank you for breakfast. I enjoyed it very much."

"So did I. Don't forget you're doing me a great favor. It was my pleasure." *I want to do it again and again.* "When you're ready, I'll turn this on."

WAS THIS A one-time happening with Luckey? Would she ever see him again? Ally wished it didn't matter, but she was so attracted to him she could hardly think about anything else.

Taking a deep breath, she looked down at the writing. She ought to be used to this after working alongside her mother in China on human trafficking cases. They'd assembled statistics about lost girls disappearing from Hunan Province for several years. But each case was heart wrenching in its own right.

Ally knew she could never be indifferent to the suffering of these young women. Thank heaven there were people invested in fighting this brand of evil, people like the bone-achingly attractive man sitting beside her. If Ally's mother were to find out about this, she'd be overjoyed to hear that the Texas Rangers had been called in to work on this case. But Ally had promised Luckey complete secrecy and she meant to uphold that promise.

"I'm ready."

He turned on the recorder. "This is James Davis of Company H, Austin, Texas, investigating the case of Jane Doe, a young Chinese girl who died March 2. It is now March 10, 10:30 a.m. Dr. Allyson Forrester Duncan, Director of Asian Studies at the University of Texas at Austin, will translate a message from the secret Nüshu language of the sworn sisters in the Hunan Province of China. It is written in the deceased's blood on the underside of the dress she was wearing when mounted police found her body dumped on an Austin street."

Shuddering over the circumstances of the poor girl's death, Ally began translating while he held the recorder.

"'Someone help us. We are being held by an evil man with a dragon's forked tongue. He smells like garlic and speaks English, Xiang and Indonesian. There are many of us imprisoned here, and other evil men speaking English come to do terrible things to us. We've been kidnapped and stolen from our homes. We don't know where we are. We miss our families. I know I am going to die. Some of the others with me have been killed already for trying to escape. There is no way out of here. Please, someone help us.'"

Ally handed him back the pages. He turned off the recorder, then rewound it and played it back so she could hear. When it was over, he clicked off and said, "That part about the men speaking English is significant. But even more so is her mention of the man who smells of garlic and speaks with a dragon's forked tongue. Those have to be clues."

"Definitely," Ally said. "We know that a forked tongue means the same thing in every language. But because she was Chinese, I would have thought she'd use the analogy of a snake. Instead, she *did* refer to the Komodo dragon, the long forked tongue of which is a deep yellow. That was an unusual thing for her to do."

"Agreed. Komodo dragons come from Indonesia," Luckey mused. "Perhaps her reference to the tongue meant he was blond haired. She said he spoke Indonesian as well as English and her native language. What is it again?"

"Xiang, which she would have spoken in Yongzhou and Changsha, but being upper-class, she would have spoken Mandarin, too."

"Thank you for doing this, Ally," he said. "The whole department is indebted to you, not to mention the parents of this girl if they can be found. Their anguish must be terrible."

Ally looked at him. Her pain went too deep for tears. "What a brave young woman to write that, knowing it would be her death sentence if she was found out. I can't even imagine her terror. How was she killed?"

"Shot in the back."

"Probably trying to escape a situation she couldn't bear a second longer."

"No doubt," he muttered. "Ally? Are you free for a while longer?"

His question quickened her pulse. Whether he'd asked her that because of the case or for another reason, it didn't matter. She didn't want to have to say goodbye to him this morning. "Yes."

"Will you follow me to the morgue? I want to show you the dress from the evidence room. I hope it won't distress you too much, but something you said about this woman being of the higher class has given me an idea I want to explore."

Ally didn't have to think. "I've wanted to see the real article all along."

"It's not a pretty sight."

"I'm not worried about that. After what that girl went through, if there's anything I can do to help you find her killer and have her body shipped back to her parents, I'll do it." But identifying her sounded next to impossible.

He gave Ally the address in case they got separated, then slid out of her car and got into a Volvo parked at the other end of the lot. Her heart pounded against her rib cage all the way downtown, where she parked her car next to his in front of the coroner's office.

Luckey's eyes searched hers with concern after she got out. "Are you sure you're all right doing this?"

"Positive. During the years I helped my mother gather statistics, we always felt so helpless. But today I'm going to be doing something useful. You don't know what a good feeling that is."

"Actually I *do*," he said in his deep, attractive voice.

Of course he did, and she admired him for it.

Luckey accompanied her inside and introduced her to the coroner. "Dr. Duncan is the Chinese expert I needed for this case. Could we see inside the evidence box again?"

Dr. Wolff told them to go into his private office while he retrieved it. It wasn't long before he returned with a box of plastic gloves and another, larger box.

After they'd both donned their gloves, Luckey took off the lid of the evidence box and gently removed the garment. As he handed it to her, she saw the hole made in the back. "When you're ready to tell me anything and everything you can about the dress, I'll record you."

After studying the writing on the inside, she laid it out on the table and nodded to him. "This is a cheongsam, actually the term for a man's mandarin-style robe. Over the years it became the name of a body-hugging, one-piece women's dress that features a frog, which is a knob of intricately knotted strings. It has two big openings at either side of the hems for convenient movement, and it is often buttoned on the right side, but not always.

"The cheongsam comes in various styles based on differences in the shapes of the collar, the length of the openings, hem and the width of the sleeves. The embroidery might show a peony, a lotus flower, a dragon or fish."

Ally darted him a glance. "*This* garment is made of very expensive embroidered silk with fine gold threading, and belongs to a woman from a highborn family. The design depicts a lotus, which symbolizes purity."

Luckey eyed her intently. "Do you think that aspect is significant?"

"It could be." She smoothed the material between her fingers. "A fabric like this in pale pink is normally worn by a slim young woman, because it wouldn't look as good on a heavier woman. The hem is knee length. The short, tight sleeve indicates this female has slender arms. See this collar? It's midsize because the woman wearing this has a shorter neck. A taller woman would wear a higher collar."

"Amazing," Luckey murmured.

"The hem is midlength. Notice that the slits are just high enough to allow leg movement, indicating modesty. The dress is formfitting to reveal beautiful posture and feminine curves, and exude an air of elegance and grace." Ally stopped talking and looked up at him. "That's all the information I can think of."

He shook his head and turned off the recorder. "You sound like a forensics expert. I'm in awe of your knowledge. Do you have any idea where this cheongsam would have been purchased?"

"It was probably made by a seamstress for the family. If the embroidery is in the Xiang style, then it might have been bought at a high-end silk merchant in Jiangyong County or Yongzhou City itself."

Luckey got up from the table. "Excuse me for a minute. I'll be right back." A few minutes later he returned with the coroner, who'd brought another box with him.

"I've asked him to let you look at the clothes of the Indonesian woman." He undid the lid and pulled out an embroidered blouse. "Can you tell me anything about this?"

Ally examined it. "My friend Soo-Lin could. She and I occasionally saw an Indonesian girl at the university wearing a tight-fitting lace blouse like this with a long skirt. I remember she called it a kebaya."

Luckey nodded to the older man, who carried a pair of scissors. He cut a three-by-three-inch swatch from the backs of both outfits. "There you go." He returned the clothes to the boxes and walked out with them and the glove carton.

The Ranger wore a satisfied expression. "I've got my samples."

"I didn't know you could do that to evidence."

"You can't."

Ally averted her eyes. "Unless you're you." Because he was the best of the best.

"The next thing I need to do is track down these materials. I can't thank you enough for what you've done."

"I feel the same way about you working on this

case, so we're even." *Don't just sit here, Ally.* She checked her watch. "I'd better get going."

He pulled a business card from his pocket. After writing a phone number on the back, he handed it to her. "Ring me at either number if any other thoughts come to your mind that could help this case."

"I will, I promise."

The card with his cell phone number burned a hole in her palm. She hurried out of the office to the car, and once safely inside, looked at the card in detail. When working on a case, did he give everyone who helped him his cell number?

She drove away wishing he'd made some suggestion about seeing her again. A man like him came along only once in a lifetime. But even if he was free to date, what were the odds of him pursuing her while he was in deep, looking for a possible serial killer?

When she got home, Ally went upstairs to her room. Her parents were out, which made it the perfect time to write a letter to Soo-Lin. After grabbing a notebook and pen, Ally stretched out on her bed to read her friend's letter again before answering it. When she came to the part about Yu Tan, a cold, clammy sensation crept through her body, making her feel ill.

Three weeks ago their sixteen-year-old daughter, Yu Tan, didn't come home from school. One of her friends said she ran off with a man from a disco club in the city, where she often went dancing without permission. I don't believe it. Yu Tan is a sweet, well-brought-up young woman with plans to make the Olympic team and go to college. She's won all kinds of awards in gymnastics.

As Ally continued to read Soo-Lin's concerns about Yu Tan's disappearance, that sickness grew, until she slid off the bed to look for her purse. Inside was the card Luckey had given her with his phone number.

Maybe there was no connection between the words she'd just read and the case that Luckey was working on, but she needed to get his permission to discuss this with her parents. The news in Soo-Lin's letter had struck too close to home.

LUCKEY LEFT THE morgue with the swatches of material in his pocket and headed for the office. On his way down the hall he was relieved to see Cy coming out of the lunchroom with a mug of coffee. There was no one he'd rather talk with about this case than him. "Ranger Vance, as I live and breathe!"

Cy saw him and grinned. "Where have you been for the last couple of weeks?"

"You don't want to hear about it."

"Actually, I already did. TJ spread the word that you nailed those three felons. Grab some coffee and come in my office so we can play catch-up."

Luckey didn't need to be persuaded. In less than a minute he was sitting across from Cy at his friend's desk and sipping the hot liquid. "How's the baby?"

"She's a heartbreaker, like Kellie."

"Another champion barrel racer?"

"Maybe." He eyed Luckey. "But the important question is, how's your personal life?"

He'd been concentrating so hard on thinking about Ally Duncan, the question took him by surprise.

Cy's eyes narrowed. "What's this? Silence from our dedicated bachelor?"

After a pause he said, "Do you remember the day you bumped into Kellie outside the radio station in Bandera?"

"What kind of a question is that? You know damn well it was the greatest day of my life." His friend studied him. "Okay, buddy. You're setting me up for something. Out with it."

"I had a similar experience yesterday."

"Yeah?" Cy broke into a smile that lit up his face. "I guess I don't need to ask if she's drop-dead gorgeous."

"Nope."

He let out a yelp that filled the room and jumped out of his chair to slap Luckey on the shoulder. In the process he set down his mug so hard some of his coffee spilled. "I knew it had to happen sooner or later! Wait till the guys hear about this. What's her name?"

"Dr. Duncan."

"That has a nice ring. Where did this encounter happen?"

"At the university. She was coming out of her office and we…collided."

Cy chuckled. "I can relate and haven't been the same since. What were you doing there?"

"I needed to find an expert in Chinese to help me on my new case."

His brows lifted. "She teaches Chinese?"

"Yup. She went to the morgue with me to identify the writing on some fabric." He pulled an evidence bag from his pocket that held the samples of embroidered silk and lace. "You're looking at some swatches that are going to crack it."

"So the morgue was your first date?"

"Nope. We had breakfast at the Magnolia Café first."

"You're a dark horse, you know that?" His friend rolled his eyes. "So she's a knockout and she speaks Chinese. There's only one more important question to ask. Does she ride?"

Luckey burst into laughter. "She lives on her family's ranch, so I'm assuming as much."

"Three out of three. Now you've got my attention." Cy walked back to his chair and sat down. "All right. I want you to start over and don't leave anything out."

"Just remember, I have no idea how she feels about me."

No sooner had he spoken than his cell phone rang. Luckey pulled it out of his pocket and checked the caller ID. He couldn't believe it. Needing privacy, Luckey got up from the chair and walked out into the hall. He clicked on. "Ally?"

"Hi. Forgive me for bothering you when I know

how busy you are, but I need to discuss something really important with you. Can we meet again?"

His heart thundered in his chest. "Where are you?"

"I'm home, but I'd be glad to drive to your office if you're there."

"How soon can you get here?"

"I'll leave the house now. What's the address?"

He gave her the information. "I'm on the second floor when you come up the stairs. Third door on the left."

"Thank you. I'll be there shortly."

After hanging up, he walked back into Cy's office.

"Was that who I think it was?"

Luckey took a deep breath. "Yes. She's on her way here to discuss something important about the case."

Cy was all smiles as he cleaned up the coffee spill. "Sure she is. What was it you said? Something like 'I don't know how she feels about me'? She's doing both of us a favor, because I want to get a good look at her."

Luckey shook his head. "She sounded serious."

"While you wait for her, tell me why you need a Chinese expert."

"It's a female trafficking case involving a Chinese victim."

For the next little while, he told him what he'd uncovered and they talked about possible theories. "I believe the victims are being held here in Houston or Austin or somewhere nearby. I've got to find out where."

"Don't be afraid to use me if you want help."

"Thanks, Cy. I might take you up on it."

He got up and went out into the hall to keep watch for Ally. The office was busy, with lots of staff milling around, but she was impossible to miss when she appeared at the top of the stairs. She was wearing the same outfit she'd worn to breakfast. "You got here fast," he said, walking toward her.

She sounded a little out of breath. "The traffic cooperated."

"Come with me."

Cy had just emerged from his office with the empty coffee mug. Luckey slowed down. "Ally? I'd like you to meet a friend and colleague Cy Vance."

A smile broke out on her face. "Another famous Ranger. I always wanted to meet one. Now I've met two." She shook his hand.

"Even if the famous part is fiction, that's the nicest thing anyone has said to us in a long time." Luckey saw the way Cy's eyes lit up. "It's a pleasure to meet you. I'm on my way for more coffee. Do either of you want some?"

"Not for me, but thank you," she said.

Luckey flashed him a private glance. "We're good. Talk to you later." He turned to Ally. "My office is right down here."

He showed her inside and shut the door. "Have a seat."

"Thank you for meeting with me again so soon."

"When I'm on a case, I don't let anything interfere with my work." Luckey sat down behind his desk. "Tell me what's happened."

"During the years we lived in China, our family

was watched by the Ministry of State Security. The MSS employs a variety of tactics including cyber spying to gain access to sensitive information. They also engage in industrial espionage. Because of this, I was never allowed to use email or the phone.

"As I told you, Soo-Lin and I met and became friends at the university. Any news passed back and forth had to be done in person, either at school, my parents' home or when I traveled to her home in Yongzhou. When I went there on vacation, I didn't contact my parents at all during my stay in order to avoid a paper or electronic trail. The MSS is always looking for subversive chatter."

Luckey marveled over her family's ability to function under such difficult conditions. "That couldn't have been easy."

"I got used to it. But when our family came back to the States, it meant I had to resort to using my father in order to correspond with her. He's constantly sending classified material to the new ambassador and receiving classified information back through the diplomatic pouch. When Soo-Lin has a letter for me, she takes the train to Changsha and leaves it with a trusted professor at the university who became our good friend.

"He comes from an old, venerable family. One of his sons works at the American Embassy in Beijing and facilitates our exchange of mail now that I'm in the States. What he does is put Soo-Lin's letters in the diplomatic pouch for my father. If I've sent a letter in the pouch, he gives it to his grandfather, who passes it off to Soo-Lin when she visits the university. Father reminded me we have to be careful after what happened to the artist Ai Weiwei."

Luckey stirred in the chair. "I read he was detained for months and interrogated fifty times for being openly critical of the Chinese government's stance on democracy and human rights. I remember hearing that the officers watched him in his sleep, their faces inches from his."

She nodded. "He was finally released but is still under their watch. His story is common. Even though our family is back in the States, because of my mother's work against trafficking we have to be extra careful. But we're willing to take the risk. Yesterday my dad flew in from DC and brought Soo-Lin's latest letter to me. You won't be able to read it, so I'll translate the important part for you."

Ally withdrew it from her purse and started reading. As Luckey listened, he was reminded of what Dr. Wolff told him about the latest body in the morgue. He'd said the young woman was likely either a ballerina or a gymnast. More than ever Luckey recognized the implications and understood the horror her friend's news had raised in Ally's mind. He dealt with the dark side of life every day. But now this case had become personal, because it directly affected this woman's life, a woman who had already impacted him in a profound way.

He sat forward. "You were right to bring this to me."

She stared at him through those beautiful, shadowed eyes. "Do I have your permission to tell my parents about this? They have no idea you came to see me at the university. But they love Soo-Lin and her family. When they read what's in this letter, my father won't wait to do something about it."

"That's what has me worried, Ally. Would you set up a time when I can meet with you and your parents?"

"Yes," she said softly. Before he could blink, she got up from the chair and hurried over to the door. Before exiting it, she said, "I'll drive home now. I'll phone you when it's arranged. Thank you, Luckey." Her voice throbbed.

After she'd disappeared, Cy strolled into his office. "I can tell from the look on your face you're a goner. No wonder. She's gorgeous."

Luckey tightened his jaw. "Her family is involved in a risky activity that could endanger their close friends in China."

"I haven't been assigned another case yet. Anything I can do to help?"

"Okay, come with me while I go talk to TJ. This case has just taken on a life of its own."

Chapter Three

When Ally got back she found her mother in the kitchen starting dinner. It was three thirty.

"Hi, darling. Where have you been? We drove over to see your uncle Nick. When we got home, you weren't here. I thought you didn't have to go to the university for a while."

"I went out, but not to the campus. Mom, I have something to tell you and Dad. Where is he?"

"Out talking to Hank about getting the horses vaccinated."

"It's that time of year," Ally said, but her mind was on Luckey. "Mom? Do you have any special plans tonight?"

"No. Your father wants peace and quiet. We just want our family to be together. I'm fixing a salad and his favorite baked beans. We'll barbecue some steaks."

"Would you mind if I invited someone to join us?"

Her mother pondered the question. "You're being very mysterious, rushing in here all out of breath. It must be a man to have created this unusual behavior in you."

"He's not just any man. His name is James Davis, but he goes by the nickname Luckey. He's a Texas Ranger," she said, feeling her face burn. It was embarrassing, because her mother could always see through her.

"Let me guess. Tall? Handsome? Honorable? Nothing but silver bullets in his gun and a black domino mask made from his brother's vest?"

"Mom...!" She tried to give her mother an incredulous look, but couldn't hide the grin on her face.

"So I'm right."

"Except for the mask, and maybe the bullets."

"Do you think I could ever forget your childhood hero? The Lone Ranger was your obsession when you were little." She smiled. "All right. No more teasing. How did you meet this paragon?"

"He came to my office yesterday looking for help with a case he was working on. He thinks talking to you and Dad would be very useful. But before I say any more, I need to call him. Maybe he won't be able to come this evening. Be right back." She dashed up to her room and phoned his cell.

He answered on the third ring. "Ally?"

"Hello again. I hope I'm not interrupting anything."

"Not at all. I just got out of a meeting with my boss and am headed home."

Hearing his deep voice sent a thrill through her. "I talked to my mother and told her you'd been to see me at the university on an investigation. She has no idea why, but when I told her you wanted to talk to her and Dad, she said you're welcome to come over this evening for dinner. We're having steaks on the patio. Very casual and low-key. But if tonight isn't good for you, I'm sure we can arrange another time that's more convenient."

"The timing couldn't be better," he said without hesitation. A big smile broke out on her face. "When would you like me to be there?"

"Is six all right? My dad likes to eat early when he's home."

"I'm salivating already."

Her stomach flipped over. "Good."

"Where do you live?"

Ally gave him the address on Crystal Mountain Road.

"The gray stone-and-wood ranch house sitting at the top of the canyon?"

"You've seen it?"

"From a helicopter. You live in prime horse country."

"The Duncans have been ranching people for three generations. My dad was a cowboy who married my cowgirl mom before he went into the marines."

"How did he end up being ambassador to China?"

"The commandant requested two marine officers to be assigned to the navy's program for the study of Chinese, a project originally developed in the early 1900s. He ended up studying with several Chinese tutors. His Mandarin was so good that he was called in to work for US Intelligence and one thing led to another. But he's planning to retire and be a full-time rancher again at the end of the summer."

"I look forward to talking to him. See you in a little while."

Ally removed her leather cord, she headed for the bathroom to shower. After toweling off, she dressed in jeans and a navy crewneck sweater. She slipped on her tan wedge sandals. This wasn't a real date. Luckey was working a case, but her heart didn't know the difference, because he was coming to the ranch and she could hardly wait to see him again.

After giving her hair a quick brush and applying a coat of pink gloss lipstick, she was ready. She pulled the letter from Soo-Lin out of her purse, went downstairs and found her parents out on the patio off the kitchen, drinking iced tea. Her dad had stretched out on a lounger in his cowboy boots.

"Sorry I took so long. What a great help I am!" Ally saw that her mom had already brought out the food and plates to the serving table.

"Don't worry about it."

"You look lovely," her father said. "I understand we're expecting a Texas Ranger for dinner."

"Yes. I told him to be here at six. But before he gets here, you and Mom should see this."

Ally handed her dad the letter and watched his face darken as he read it. Wordlessly, he handed it to her mother, who was proficient in Chinese, too. She started to read it. "Poor Soo-Lin. I know how much she wanted a baby."

"It breaks my heart, but the other news is even sadder. Keep reading."

After a minute, her mother cried out, "Oh, no—not Yu Tan!"

"Horrible, isn't it?" Ally said. "But I don't believe the story about her running off with a man."

"Neither do I," her father muttered.

"Because Luckey sought me out at the university yesterday needing help on a case involving female trafficking, I showed him this letter today."

Her father sat up with a grim look on his face. "Why would you do that?"

"Please don't be upset, Dad. Oh—there's the doorbell. I'll let him tell you the whole story."

Her mother jumped up from her chair. "But not before we eat. Larry? Will you start the steaks?"

Ally walked through the house. The second she opened the door and saw Luckey dressed in a black sport shirt and gray chinos, her legs turned to mush. "You made it. Come in."

"It's gorgeous country up here." His dark brown eyes enveloped her as he said it, sending a curl of warmth through her body. Only then did she notice the file folder under his arm.

"Follow me. We're out on the patio."

Ally made introductions and her mother handed Luckey a glass of iced tea. They chatted about casual things before filling their plates and seating themselves around the wrought-iron table to eat.

"These beans are out of this world, Mrs. Duncan," he said, causing her mom to beam.

"Thank you. It's an old family recipe."

"Is that steak done the way you like it, Luckey?" Ally's father asked.

"It's perfect."

"We've never had a Texas Ranger for dinner before. You've made my daughter's night," he added. "When she was a little girl, she was crazy about the Lone Ranger."

Oh, no.

Luckey's gaze swerved to hers. "Is that right?"

"We bought her a pony she named Silver. She must have had half a dozen black masks." Her dad was on a roll. "I think there are still a couple of them out in the tack room left over from the good old days."

"Those I've got to see," Luckey said.

Ally cleared her throat, eager to change the subject. "Luckey? Why don't you tell my parents why you came to my office yesterday?"

With those words, the atmosphere around the table changed. Luckey got up from the table to get the file folder he'd left on one of the loungers. After he sat down again, he passed around the pages with the photos of the Chinese writing and explained where they'd come from.

For the next twenty minutes he discussed the case he'd been assigned and the information he'd gleaned from forensics. Her parents didn't say a word. They were too busy absorbing everything he was telling them.

"Your work fighting the trafficking program hasn't gone unnoticed, Mrs. Duncan. Your name came up at a conference I attended a month ago, praising your efforts."

"Thank you," she said.

"Ally tells me she's helped you when she could. That's why she brought Soo-Lin's letter to me. When I read about the disappearance of the young woman who hoped to be an Olympic gymnast one day, it reminded me of something Dr. Wolff told me at the morgue. He said the victim's body indicated she was probably either a dancer or a gymnast."

A gasp escaped Ally. She eyed her parents, who looked equally stunned.

"I'm not assuming that the dead girl is the girl your family knows. If I showed all of you her picture, would you recognize her?"

"No," Ally said at once. "It's been nine years since we were at the wedding. She was only seven at the time. But if Soo-Lin saw the photo you have, I'm sure she would know one way or the other."

"That's good to know, and we can explore that avenue later." He eyed her parents. "Ally examined the dress and described the special elements to me. She said it had probably been made rather than bought for a girl of the higher class. If I could find out where that material came from, I might be able to discover who bought it and had the dress made. That could lead me to the girl's parents."

"And you could unite them with their child," Beatrice said. "What a blessing it would be if you could do that."

Luckey eyed Ally. "Do you know if the Tan girl learned the Nüshu language?"

She shook her head. "But Soo-Lin would know."

Ally's father got up from the table and walked around for a minute. "Dad? What are you thinking?"

He turned to them. "I'm thinking I need to make another trip to China."

"No, Larry. You're not the ambassador anymore and another visit would be monitored the second you get off the plane in Beijing."

"Mom's right, Dad. But *I* could make a quick trip to Yongzhou to see Soo-Lin."

"Absolutely not," her father said sternly.

"Then with Luckey's permission, we could send that swatch in a letter to Soo-Lin in the usual way."

Her father shook his head. "Having learned about all this, we mustn't put your teacher or his son in any more danger. It puts the embassy itself at risk. I shouldn't have allowed it to continue after we left China. So, no more using the diplomatic pouch. For the time being you'll have to stop corresponding with Soo-Lin. If Yu Tan was indeed kidnapped, I don't want the lives of the Tan family further jeopardized until there can be an investigation."

Ally felt sick. "How long do I have to wait to write her back?"

"At least until fall, when I'm no longer working for the government. Then we'll see if we can find a different way to contact her."

"If I may say something," Luckey interjected.

He'd gotten to his feet with the file he'd brought. "I need to leave, but before I go let me assure you I have my own methods to track down the material. It's not my only lead and I have other ideas I'm working on. I'm confident I'll be able to find out the name of the girl in the morgue and inform her parents, if they can be found. If it should turn out the girl is Yu Tan—"

"Then her father will say she didn't dishonor their family," Ally interrupted, with bitterness in her voice. "That will mean more to him than the fact that she was murdered."

Her mother stood up and started clearing the table. "There are too many Chinese girls missing from their families. Bless you for the part you're playing in this, Ranger Davis."

"Amen," her husband said, and shook Luckey's hand.

"It's been an honor to meet all of you. Thank you for the delicious dinner."

The night was ending.

Ally took a deep breath. "I'll see you out." Her heart sank to her feet as she and Luckey walked through the ranch house to the front door. After she opened it, he turned to her. "Despite the tragic circumstances we talked about tonight, I had a great time."

"So did I," she said.

His eyes danced over her features. "I'll be in touch soon. Good night, Ally."

"Good night."

She closed the door, not ready to see him walk away, but there was nothing she could do about it. Needing an outlet, she returned to the kitchen to help her parents do the dishes. Her father smiled at her. "Your Ranger is the reason they're still legendary."

"He's even more handsome than your childhood movie idol," her mom added.

"I'm afraid he's not *my* Ranger, but I agree he's pretty amazing." She finished loading the dishwasher. "While you're both still up, there's something else I need to tell you. The case he's working on involves more than one victim."

Both of them looked surprised.

"He told me that the bodies of three other young women, Chinese and Indonesian, have been dumped on the streets of Austin over the last ten months."

"Ally!" her mother gasped.

"The one wearing the cheongsam was killed a week ago. When the police couldn't find the person or persons responsible, they turned it over to the Texas Rangers and Luckey was assigned. It's his opinion that the crimes are related and the women were possibly murdered by the same killer or ring of killers. Since he has access to the paperwork from the morgue, here's what I'm thinking.

"Mom? Could I make a copy of the list of missing girls we assembled in China and give it to him? With his special resources, he could check the photographs in your files against the photos of the victims in the morgue. I know it's iffy, but maybe it will help him. What do you think? I trust him with my life."

Her parents looked at each other, and her father nodded. "It would be a start in the right direction."

"Tell you what, darling. Let's go to the den and I'll print out what we have on the computer for you to give to him," Beatrice offered.

Ally had never loved them as much as she did in that moment. "Thank you so much!" she said, kissing them both on the cheek.

She couldn't wait to give him the information. It would be the excuse she needed to see him again. Already he was so important to her, she couldn't imagine life without him.

WEDNESDAY MORNING LUCKEY got started early and met Randy at the site where he'd found the body last week. His brother had copies of the crime scene photos with him, and the two scoured the area, trying to see if the detective had overlooked any evidence that could help identify the car involved in the drop.

After that, Luckey met with the police officers who'd found the other three bodies. They walked around the crime scenes. He'd hoped to find something that had escaped the forensics team, but didn't come up with any new evidence.

En route to work he phoned the lab at headquarters. "Stan? What have you got for me on that DMSO cream used by athletes?"

"Wish I could help you out, but no brand on the

market in the US matches the evidence. It had to be manufactured in a foreign country. Where do you want me to look?"

Luckey made a mental list. "Indonesia, China and Japan, for starters."

"For starters, huh? You're funny."

"I know. It's like looking for one particular grain of sand on the beach."

"I'll get on it, but it's going to take time."

"I know," he repeated. "Thanks."

He clicked off, only to accept an incoming call on his car phone. "This is Ranger Davis."

"Luckey?"

Only one woman had that slightly breathless voice. Ally had been on his mind throughout the night. He'd planned to call her later in the day, but to his delight she'd come to him.

"Would you believe I was about to phone you?"

"That relieves my guilt for bothering you once again."

He drew a sharp breath. "In case you've forgotten, I invaded your office on Monday."

"That was our family's lucky day."

Luckey was happy to accept that collective compliment. But he was waiting for the moment when it became more personal.

"I'm calling to find out if you'd like a copy of my mother's work on female trafficking that she compiled while we were in China. She has names, addresses, descriptions of lost girls and in some cases photos, all from areas in the Jingjinji metropolitan region and the Hunan Province. I was thinking—"

"You were thinking maybe one of the photos might match one of the girls in the morgue?" he interrupted.

"Yes."

"It's entirely possible. That would be a real gift for the department. Are your parents on board with this?"

"I wouldn't have offered it otherwise."

"No. I'm sure you wouldn't. Where are you going to be this afternoon?"

"I'm helping out at the orphanage that brings in special-needs children from China and finds them homes here."

"One of your father's projects?"

"Yes," she said quietly. "He got the foundation started a long time ago, through friends and donors."

Why wasn't Luckey surprised? Her family was amazing. As for Ally… "What time will you be through?"

"At five."

"Why don't I meet you there." He wanted to see the orphanage and find out the backgrounds of the staff who worked there, but he'd talk to Ally about it when the time seemed right. "Then we can decide on a restaurant to go for dinner and I'll look through the information. Tell me the address." When she'd given it to him, he said, "You've made my day. See you this evening."

The rest of the afternoon he made phone calls to silk merchants in several of the big cities in Texas, until he located a fabric store called Hui's, in Houston. The employee who answered the phone explained that they got their silk fabric from a Chinese merchant who traveled from their main outlet in Beijing every other month. He happened to be in Houston right now. Luckey made arrangements to meet with him the next day.

With that accomplished, he'd done as much as he could on the case today. Tonight he'd be having dinner with the woman who'd captured his attention the moment she'd accidentally run into his arms. He couldn't think about anything else.

After stopping in at home to take a quick shower, he drove to Barton Creek and looked for the historic home on Maravillas Loop that had been converted into an orphanage. As he pulled up in front, he saw Ally sitting on a porch swing holding a toddler-aged girl in her arms. He got out of the car and started up the pathway to the door. That was when he noticed a young Asian woman in a chair next to the swing.

"We're glad you're here," Ally said. "Meet Shan. She works with the day shift." He shook the timid woman's hand and was surprised to see bruising on her arms. "And this is little Bu. She has cystic fibrosis, but it can be managed with the right care."

"How do you say 'hi' to her?"

"Ni hao."

Luckey tried it. The little girl didn't respond, but stared hard at him. "Her parents couldn't keep her?"

"I don't know the whole story, but she's precious."

Ally kissed both her cheeks and said something in Chinese. It was the first time he'd heard her speak

the language. The little girl said something back and
started to cry. Clearly, she didn't want Ally to go. The
tender scene pulled on his heartstrings.

Ally turned the girl over to the other woman, who
looked to be about nineteen or twenty.

"Let's go before she has a meltdown." Ally reached
for her purse and a loose-leaf binder that had been on
the swing beside her. She and Luckey walked down
the steps together.

"Where's your car?"

"Around the side."

"We'll go in my car and I'll bring you back later."
When they reached it, he opened the door for her,
then got behind the wheel. "Ally? One of the penal-
ties you have to pay for being with me means I've got
this latest case on my mind. Sometime soon will you
do me a favor and let me see the orphanage books? I
need to make a list of all the Chinese people who've
worked or still work there."

She looked alarmed. "What are you thinking?"

He took a deep breath. "I'm anxious to track down
as many young Chinese women as I can, in case
they're in trouble. If any of the employees here are tied
up in any way as part of this trafficking ring, maybe
one of them will recognize the girls in the morgue.
I'm acting on every lead possible."

"I'll talk to my father."

"Thank you." He pulled onto the main street.
"Now that we have that out of the way, what are you
in the mood for?"

"Anything."

He smiled. "Then let's go to The Grove and sit on the deck."

"I love that place. All those huge trees."

"The Italian food isn't bad, either."

Before long they reached the restaurant and were shown to a table. Once the waitress took their orders, Ally handed him the binder. He thanked her for it, but didn't open it.

"When I get home tonight, I'll spend hours digesting this. But right now I want to ask you a question." She looked so beautiful in her filmy, short-sleeved blouse and white skirt. He hadn't been able to miss the fact that every guy who walked past their table openly checked her out.

"What's that?"

"Is there an important man in your life? Am I treading on any toes?"

Her eyes seemed to turn a deeper blue. "No."

"Not even someone back in China?"

"I dated several American men while I was there. There was one I was pretty serious about. His name was Jack Reynolds. He was a judge advocate in the Marines Corps, working in international and operational law. I came close to marrying him."

"Why didn't you?"

"It would have meant living all over the world. I'm afraid I'm a Texas girl at heart, despite spending so many years overseas. When you asked me why I didn't stay in China with my friends, the truth is, I was homesick for the ranch."

"Did you have opportunities to ride over there?"

"Yea, but it wasn't the same. Hunan Province has great beauty, but it doesn't have hot spots of bluebonnets you can't wait to run through. We always came home in April so we wouldn't miss them in bloom."

"I take it you're happy to be home," Luckey murmured. The dreamy expression on her face said it all, and a vision filled his mind. He could see her riding through purple-blue fields with the wind blowing her lustrous black hair back from her face.

"Oh, yes. I'm never leaving again, except to go on vacation."

While her pronouncement trickled through Luckey's awareness like mist, exciting him, the waitress brought their dinner.

"I'm a Texas man myself."

Ally flashed him a smile that blew him away. "I would never have guessed. Since we're exchanging information, are you involved with someone who wouldn't like it that you're having dinner with me tonight? Even if it is because of the case you're investigating?"

He put down his fork. "For me it stopped being about this case the moment you opened your office door and we ran into each other. Does that answer your question?"

"Not all of them," she said unexpectedly. Her smile had faded. "If you told me you'd never been in love, I wouldn't believe you."

"I fell hard for a woman in college and married her. We were both twenty-two. But when I was taken on as a Ranger, our problems began. I thought she understood what it meant, but I was naive. Within two years we divorced, and she went back to Houston, where she lives now with her new husband and two kids. He sells insurance, a nine-to-five man."

"Not every woman could handle what you do for a living. I was surprised my mother could handle the life she shared with my father."

Luckey was extremely interested in the answer to his next question. "What do you think was the key?"

"When I asked her, she said, 'Ally? I fell in love with a cowboy and that never changed, because no job can ever take the cowboy out of a real man.'"

"Your mother sounds a lot like mine."

Ally cocked her head. "In what way?"

"Both my parents came from ranching families who've done it for generations. Dad was a rancher before he became a police officer and eventually the sheriff of Travis County. Mom got her nursing degree. Last year they both retired and are back to full-time ranching."

"Where?"

"In Dripping Springs."

"That's only half an hour away. How nice that you can be close to your family. I bet your mom loves it. Are you an only child like me?"

"No. I have a younger brother, Randy. He's on the police force here in Austin."

"Law enforcement is alive and doing well in the Davis blood. Didn't he want to be a Ranger, too?"

Luckey nodded. "It's odd you'd say that. Randy

hopes to be taken on next year. He's married and has two little girls."

"Do you have lots of extended family?"

"Lots. They all live in Dripping Springs. What about you?"

"I have my share, too. Some of our relatives lived on our ranch for different periods while we were away, to keep watch over everything."

"That's the beauty of a large family." They'd finished eating. "My twenty questions are over. With that discussion concluded, what do you say we go get your car? I'll follow you home."

"Sure. Sounds good."

The whole time they were driving to the orphanage, and after, on his way to her house, Luckey had a hard time believing that this was really happening. He could thank providence that TJ had let him take this trafficking case. If it hadn't been for Randy and their conversation about the dumped body, Luckey would probably have picked the case of the wheelchair-bound victim who'd been set on fire.

His grandfather had used a wheelchair before his death. The possibility of him being murdered that way didn't bear thinking about. In any event, Luckey couldn't comprehend not knowing Ally now.

He could hardly believe that, after all these years of being alone, he'd met a woman who'd managed, without even trying, to break through the wall he'd built around himself. She brought out every male instinct in him. Thank heaven her father had forbidden her to travel back to China. At this point Luckey's protective instincts were on full alert. No matter how much she cared about her friend, one wrong move and Ally could disappear. He'd known her only a few days, but that didn't matter. He wanted her in his life.

She drove fast. He liked that.

By the time they reached her house, twilight had turned into night. He jumped out of his car and walked around to hers. She'd just turned off the engine. Luckey wanted to pull her out of the car into his arms and take her home with him, but of course he couldn't do that. In fact, he didn't dare touch her yet, fearing he wouldn't be able to stop.

Fighting his desire, he opened the door so she could climb out. It was impossible not to notice her shapely legs in the tight, knee-length skirt she wore.

"Thank you for dinner, Luckey."

Their bodies were close enough that he could feel the heat between them. "I enjoyed our evening. Please tell your mother I'm in her debt and yours for the binder you've given me. I'll be poring over it all night. I'll get it back to you soon."

"No, no. It's yours to keep."

He still didn't want to let her go. "What's your schedule like tomorrow?"

"I'll be home reading over my graduate students' theses."

"Sounds like heavy work, but you like it, right?"

"I do."

Get away from her, Davis.

"I want to see you again. Friday some of my friends are getting together for a family birthday party. You met Cy. He'll be there with his wife and daughter. Would you like to go with me?"

After a pause Ally said, "If you're asking me to a Ranger party, how could I possibly refuse?"

"Good. I'll call you sometime tomorrow and let you know the details. We'll go riding and probably roast hot dogs around a campfire."

"I haven't done that in forever. It's the reason I wanted to come home. I can't wait."

"We'll take our horses in my trailer."

"What's your horse's name?"

"Persey, after the Perseus constellation. I guess I don't need to ask the name of your horse."

"I'm embarrassed to tell you."

Luckey grinned. "Silver's a great name. Bring one of your masks, too."

"Don't you dare tell your friends about that."

"Why? It's a charming story told by a loving parent. What did you do with your pony when you left for China?"

"We stabled Silver with some neighbours."

"My friend Vic will be there with his wife and son. Jeremy's the one having the birthday. He has a pony and a miniature horse."

"Oh…a toy horse? I'd love to see it."

"I'll give Vic a call and see if he'll bring both."

"That'll be so fun. Thank you, Luckey. Now I'd better not keep you. Good night." She hurried up the steps to her front porch and disappeared in the house.

He got back in his car, but sat there for a minute in a daze. For the first time in years he was going to go to a party with a most incredible woman.

Chapter Four

Early Friday evening, Ally watched for Luckey from the front porch of the ranch house, wearing her black cowboy hat and cowboy boots. She'd dressed in jeans and a long-sleeved black Western shirt with silver fringe. Ally was so excited to be going with him she couldn't stand still.

At four on the dot he drove up in a four-door dark red Dodge Ram 3500 truck pulling a two-horse trailer. She hurried down the steps to the vehicle, while Luckey opened the passenger door from inside so she could climb in. The gorgeous man wore a white Stetson and cowboy boots. There was no guy on earth who could equal his rugged good looks. "You're right on time!" she blurted, with too much excitement.

"I've been looking forward to this outing since the other night and don't want to miss a second of it." His eyes played over her. "Black on black. I like it. The only thing missing is your black mask."

His gaze missed nothing. She swallowed hard. "Keep winding down this road and we'll eventually come to the barn."

"I want inside that tack room. Maybe we'll find one of your masks."

Her cheeks felt warm. "Dad was just kidding."

Luckey drove past the corral to the front of the barn. After pulling to a stop, he got out to open the rear of the horse trailer.

Ally joined him. "So *this* is Persey." The horse nickered, causing her to chuckle. "You're a handsome specimen." The golden palomino had a lustrous white mane and tail and was every bit as magnificent as his owner. "I'll have to bring you some treats."

"Did you hear that?" Luckey had entered the stall to speak to his horse. "We're bringing you a girl-friend. Her name is Silver. We'll be right back." He patted his horse's rump and followed Ally into the barn.

She led him over to the stall where she kept her Morgan. Luckey's knowing eye inspected the mare. "You've got a true black Silver here. Beautiful with that silver mane and tail."

"You're my sweetheart, aren't you?" She hugged her horse's head and kissed her. "We're going on a ride with Luckey and his friends." Silver nickered. "Let me show him my gear and then I'll take care of you."

When they reached the tack room he turned to her. "I'll carry out your stuff while you load him."

Ally grabbed some Buckeye Carrot Crunchers and led her horse out to the trailer. She talked in sooth-ing tones as she walked Silver inside and gave both animals a treat. While they chomped on their goodies, Luckey came in with the gear. When he heard the noise, his deep chuckle worked its way to her insides.

"Spoiling you already, is she?" Though he'd spoken to his horse, his eyes had focused on her.

"It never hurts."

"That works for humans, too."

She tossed him a treat, making him laugh. They secured the horses and got back into the truck. "We don't have far to drive," Luckey told her. "Kit's property is out here in Barton Creek, too. After he got married, he wanted more acreage for their horses, and moved out of his condo. He and his wife are throwing this party for Jeremy."

Within minutes they arrived at the new glass-and-wood two-story house, where Ally spotted other trucks and horse trailers. Luckey escorted her inside to the big family room, where he introduced her to Kit and Natalie, who owned the house. Their little two-year-old, Amy, was adorable. Ally was envious.

"What a darling little girl, all dressed up in her Western duds," she exclaimed.

Natalie laughed. "My husband has already turned her into a cowgirl."

"My father did the same thing to me."

"He sure did." Luckey's eyes were all over Ally. Talk about legs turning to jelly!

Slowly, they circulated around the room. She'd met Cy before. He stood next to his wife, Kellie, who was holding their baby, Holly.

"Kellie is our state's most famous barrel racer," Luckey informed Ally.

"Not anymore. I'm too out of shape," she lamented.

Ally smiled. "I saw you in a rodeo on one of our trips home. You were fantastic."

Cy put an arm around his wife. "She would have won the world championship if she hadn't found out she was pregnant and had to quit the circuit."

Kellie winked at Ally. "It was his fault."

That comment drew a roar from everyone before Ally was introduced to Vic and his wife, Claire, who was in the latter stages of pregnancy.

"And this is our birthday boy," Claire said, putting her arm around a dark-haired child wearing a cowboy hat.

"Luckey told me," Ally said, handing him her gift. "Happy Birthday, Jeremy. You can go ahead and open it if you like."

The boy undid the wrapping and pulled out a red scarf.

"You know what that's a replica of," Luckey remarked. He darted her a secret glance.

"What?" Jeremy asked.

"The Lone Ranger's scarf. He wore it knotted at the side of his neck." Luckey took over and tied it for the boy.

"Cool! Thanks!" He turned to Vic. "What do you think, Dad?"

"I think that's a terrific gift for a junior Texas Ranger. All you need is a black mask to complete the outfit."

Luckey's eyes swerved to Ally's. "I know a place where I can dredge one up."

Before he had a chance to say any more, she changed the subject. "I hear you have a pony."

"Yup. His name is Comet."

"I love that name. What about your miniature horse? Is it here, too?"

He nodded. "We took them to the corral."

"I want to see both of them. I had a pony when I was young, but I never had a toy horse. They are so cute!"

"You'll love Daken."

"That's an interesting name."

"Yup. Daken is Wolverine's mutant son. It means mongrel, but my horse doesn't look like one."

Ally fought a smile. "I'm sure he doesn't. Tell me about Daken."

The boy turned to his parents. "Hey, Mom—I'm going to take her to see Comet and Daken, okay?"

"Go ahead."

"Come this way."

A grin lit up Luckey's handsome features. "While you go with him, I'll drive the horses around to the corral."

"Wonderful."

Ally opened her purse and pulled out a packet of horse treats. After setting her bag on an end table, she followed Jeremy through the house to the back door. They hurried outside to the corral. On the way, Jeremy told her all about his favorite action heroes. Living in China, she'd missed out on a lot of information important to an eight-year-old boy.

"Oh!" she cried when she saw the little brown-and-white horse playing in the grass next to the pony.

"Go sit down by him and he'll come to you."

Ally sank onto the grass and opened up the little packet of treats. Daken heard the rustle and came right over to her. She held one of the treats out on her palm and he sniffed it. Within seconds he'd gobbled it down and was stepping on her to get more. Laughter poured out of her. She lay on her side and petted him while Jeremy hunkered next to them.

"I think I have to get me a little horse, too, Jeremy." Her gaze flicked to the pony. "Uh-oh. I think Comet is jealous. I have one more treat left." She got up and walked over to the animal. "Here you go."

By now Luckey had joined them. "It appears you have everyone eating out of your hand," he told her. "How about going for a ride with me?"

A rush of warmth filled her body when she met his glance.

"Can I come?" Jeremy asked.

Luckey grinned at him. "It's your birthday, pard-ner."

"Daken will follow us."

Ally loved it. "That I've got to see."

Five minutes later Vic had saddled Jeremy's pony. The other two Rangers joined them and they all went for a ride, with Daken trailing. While they rode, Jeremy related to Ally his harrowing experience of being kidnapped from school. The story tugged on her emotions. Jeremy had no idea she'd met Luckey because he was trying to solve a horrendous kidnapping case that had ended in murder.

"Thank goodness you were found in time," she said.

"Dad charged into the room where I was tied up and took me home with him."

Ally's eyes smarted. "Aren't dads the greatest?"

"Yeah."

"Ally's dad is famous, Jeremy," Luckey said.

The boy looked up at him. "He is?"

"That's right. Years ago the president of the United States chose him to be our country's ambassador to China. Ally lived there with her family for fifteen years."

His eyes lit up. "Did you see panda bears?"

"Absolutely. My family used to go to Chengdu every fall with my friend's family. They have a panda breeding and research center there where you can see newborn panda cubs. They're so cute, just like your Daken."

"Did you have one for a pet?"

"No. I begged my father for one, but pandas are wild and owned by the People's Republic of China. It's against the law to keep one. Even if you could, you'd need to own a bamboo forest, because that's what they eat all the time."

"Daken loves grass."

"He makes a great lawnmower," Vic piped up. Everyone chuckled before he said, "I think we'd better get back, son. It's growing darker and your mom has a fun game set up for all of us out in back before we eat."

"What kind of game?"

"It's a surprise."

"Okay, let's go!"

Ally smiled at Luckey before the six of them headed back toward the ranch house. In her wildest dreams as a child, she'd never imagined riding horses with four handsome Texas Rangers.

To her delight she saw that three plastic barrels in red, white and blue had been set up in a triangle like a barrel racing event, with chairs placed around for an audience. Behind the chairs was the fire pit.

"Kellie lent Claire her practice barrels," Luckey explained.

"What a fun idea. I'd love to see her perform again."

"One day maybe."

"It's about time!" Claire called out with a smile. "We're going to have a timed contest to see who can go around the barrels the fastest. I've got a stopwatch. Come over to the table and pick out your starting number from the cowboy hat. Jeremy? Bring Daken so he'll stay by me."

"Yay!" Jeremy dismounted and hurried over to pick out a number. Daken followed and she tied the small animal to her chair.

"Hey. I'm number three!" the boy announced excitedly.

One by one the partygoers drew their numbers. "I got five," Ally told Jeremy.

"Who's first?" Claire asked.

"Luckey's my name," Luckey said as he got back on his horse. The sight of him in his cowboy gear, sitting astride his palomino, almost overwhelmed Ally. He walked his mount to the starting point.

"I'm clocking you. Ready, get set, *go!*"

Ally sucked in her breath as Luckey rounded the first two barrels with ease. But he missed the third and was disqualified. Next went Kit, who showed expert horsemanship, but his horse hit two of the barrels, disqualifying him, as well. Jeremy rode his pony next, trying hard to keep his animal focused. It was hilarious. But he didn't miss the barrels and didn't hit them.

Vic started out with a flawless performance until the second barrel, when his horse shied away in a different direction and was ruled out of the competition.

Then it was Ally's turn. She'd never barrel raced before and it showed. Hands down, she gave the worst performance of all the contestants, bumping every barrel, and was disqualified. But it was all done in good fun for Jeremy's birthday.

Last but not least came Cy, who started out well, but leaned too close at the third barrel. The momentum sent it rolling across the meadow and he had to chase after it and bring it back. With him out of the competition, the winner was clear. Luckey smiled at Ally as Claire stood up to make the announcement.

"And the gold buckle goes to Jeremy Malone for a winning time of 22 seconds!" Everyone clapped as she handed him his prize. "Great job!" She hugged and kissed him before they all congratulated him.

"Okay, guys. We've got hot dogs to cook. The buns and condiments are over on the table and there's coffee, too. For dessert we're having s'mores."

"Yum!" Jeremy exclaimed.

The bonfire provided the perfect backdrop for Ally to study Luckey's rock-solid silhouette. While the horses grazed, everyone gathered around the fire to eat. Luckey found a stick for her and they cooked their hot dogs side by side.

"You and your Ranger friends acted like you honestly tried to do your best in that race. It's so sweet of you to make this night so special for Jeremy. He seems like a great kid. I can't believe he was kidnapped."

"It was a nightmare, but Claire, who was his nanny at the time, helped find him fast. Vic married her soon after that." Luckey shook his head. "I'd like to find the guy who stole the life from those four Asian girls. The sooner the better."

"I want that, too, Luckey."

After a wonderful evening, they said goodbye to the others and loaded up for the drive back to Ally's parents' ranch. On the way there Luckey said, "You were a hit with everyone, especially Jeremy."

"I'm flattered that he asked me to come to his parents' house so I could play with Daken. What a cute boy."

"The Lone Ranger scarf was the best present you could have given him."

She glanced at the man sitting next to her. "You have great friends. I've never had a better time,

Luckey. After a night like this, I'm so glad I'm back in Texas."

"Glad enough to spend part of tomorrow with me? That is, if you don't have work."

"If this has to do with the case, then I can do both."

"What if this didn't have anything to do with it?"

Her heart stopped. "It wouldn't matter, but I think that's a trick question."

He chuckled. "It should come as no shock to you that I'd like to spend every day with you. How's that for honesty?" Ally could hardly breathe. "But as it happens, I'd like you with me tomorrow when I drive to Houston. I have an appointment with a Chinese silk merchant from Beijing whom I'm hoping might be able to shed some light on the fabric sample I have. You might be able to get more information out of him by speaking to him in his native language. Do you mind?"

"You know I don't."

"Good. I'll come pick you up at eight thirty. The appointment is for one. I thought we'd stop for lunch on the way."

They arrived at the ranch house too soon. He drove back to the barn and opened the trailer door to unload Silver. Both horses nickered. Luckey smiled at Ally in the moonlight. "I do believe they were saying good-night."

"He probably asked her for a date," Ally said with a grin.

"Yup. Persey takes after me when he sees something he wants."

Hot faced, she led her horse out of the trailer into the barn and undid the saddle. Luckey removed the bridle and carried everything to the tack room. She'd just watered her horse and filled the hay net when she felt two hands slide to her shoulders from behind.

"I had the time of my life tonight, Ally." In the next instant, Luckey pulled her back against him and kissed the side of her neck. The motion knocked off her cowboy hat, but she hardly noticed, because the touch of his lips sent shock waves through her body. He turned her around, still holding on to her arms. But his features had a haunted cast.

"I'm moving too fast and know it. Tell me now if you want to change your mind about going with me tomorrow. The truth is, I want to kiss you into tomorrow, but that's crossing a big line. I shouldn't be doing this so soon, even if I wasn't a Texas Ranger trying to obey rules."

He leaned over to scoop up her Stetson. "Come on." He put it on her head with care. "Let's get back to the truck and I'll drop you off in front of the house."

They left the barn and drove past the corral to the front drive. If Luckey only knew she was much more out of control than he was… Ally ached to be held in his arms and kissed until nothing else mattered. But he was right. It *was* too soon to give in to her feelings for him. Once she did, she'd never be the same again. What would happen if things didn't work out between them? The thought of him not being in her world frightened her.

The second he pulled to a stop, she opened the

door. "Don't bother to see me in, Luckey. I need to talk to my father about the orphanage books before he goes to bed. Thank you for taking me to the party. I'll be ready at eight thirty. Good night."

She hurried inside the house. It wasn't until after she closed the front door that she heard his truck drive away, and she wanted to cry for him to come back.

"Ally?" her mother called out from the family room.

"Yes. I'm home." She walked in to find her parents watching TV.

"How was the party?"

She took off her cowboy hat. "Great." Too great to talk about. If she got started, it would make Luckey sound too important. "Dad? Would it be possible for Luckey to look at the books on the orphanage?"

Her father appeared puzzled. "Why?"

"He picked me up at the orphanage Wednesday and wonders if there are any young Chinese women working there who might be caught in a trafficking ring and could identify the girls in the morgue. Luckey's checking out every possibility. He'll need names, ages and home addresses."

"I would never have thought of that, but it appears he's leaving no stone unturned in this investigation. Good for him. I'll go over there tomorrow and get the books."

"Thanks, Dad."

Her mother eyed her thoughtfully. "Are you going to see him again?"

"Yes. Tomorrow we're driving to Houston. He has

an appointment with a Chinese silk merchant and wants my help for translation."

And once the case was solved... *Will his infatuation wear off after he kisses the daylights out of me? Will he want to see me anymore?*

He'd been divorced a long time. She got the feeling marriage was the last thing on his mind. But where he was concerned, marriage was the only thing on hers.

"I'm going up to bed. See you in the morning. Love you," Ally said, and left the room to go upstairs.

She knew she was madly in love, for the first time in her life. She'd go anywhere that James Luckey Davis of Company H wanted to take her.

No wonder she hadn't accepted Jack Reynolds's proposal back in China. The feelings she'd had for him had everything to do with thinking it was time she got married and little to do with actual love. When it came down to it, she couldn't say yes. After meeting Luckey, she now knew why.

Chapter Five

Luckey walked his horse into the barn to get him settled for the night. "Sorry all the fun is over, Persey. I know how you feel. I had to say good-night to my girlfriend, too." He put the gear away in the tack room before putting out some fresh hay and water.

"To think you and I have been chugging along just fine these last few years and then those two turn up out of the blue to disrupt our lives. I don't know what in the hell to do about it. The hands-off approach didn't work too well tonight. How am I going to handle spending all day with her tomorrow and still stay within TJ's bounds of propriety?" Forget his own bounds, which were nonexistent after tonight.

You don't have to take her to Houston with you.

Yes, he did.

Not being able to see her wasn't an option.

He rubbed Persey's forelock. "Good night, pal."

Once inside the house he washed his hands and grabbed a soda. Much as he'd love a cup of coffee, he knew it would keep him awake. After pulling Ally close against him earlier and breathing in her scent, he didn't need any more stimulation tonight.

Before going to bed he checked his email for any department business. His family rarely emailed. They preferred to text.

The daily updates and news flashes filled the screen. He kept scrolling until he saw Headquarters Forensics Lab in the subject line. Had Stan found something already? Excitement filled Luckey as he opened it, not surprised the older man had started his message without preamble.

What are you? Some kind of supersleuth? That particular DMSO cream is manufactured through Pharma PT Gema in Jakarta, Indonesia. It's not made in great amounts and can only be purchased through mail order. It claims to be a solution for sports lovers who wish to remain active without fear of joint or muscular pain.

The FDA in the States hasn't approved it except for stem cell research, etc. One interesting side note: in some men, especially, it can cause a garlic-like body odor and taste that can be very pungent.

Luckey's breath caught. The victim who'd written her plea for help in her own blood had mentioned that her captor smelled of garlic. That had to be why.

Luckey wrote Stan back, thanking him for *his* genius in finding the manufacturer so fast.

Next he found the Gema company web page on the internet. They advertised their various products and used international express mail carriers for delivery of their goods. Armed with that information, Luckey phoned TJ and explained where his investigation had taken him. He asked for two favors.

First, he needed TJ to contact the Jakarta authorities, who would order the Gema staff to cooperate with Luckey to pinpoint the man who'd ordered the product. Second, he wanted TJ to get a warrant so he could search the records of merchandise that had been received in Austin from Gema through carriers such as FedEx, DHL or UPS, in order to track the recipient's name and address.

Once TJ assured him he'd take care of it, Luckey called Gema's contact number and told the receptionist that he was phoning on a serious police matter and needed to speak with the head of the company ASAP. The person on the other end said she would pass on the message to her superiors. Luckey couldn't wait to find an address on the purchaser, who was likely also the same person who'd killed the last victim, if not all four women.

The night couldn't pass fast enough for him.

After his shower the next morning, he dressed in a checked, button-down shirt and jeans. Once he'd eaten breakfast he put Persey out in the corral to graze. With the house locked up, Luckey left in his Volvo to go pick up Ally. His pulse raced just thinking about her.

When he reached the ranch and she opened the door to him, she looked good enough to eat. He knew it was an overused expression, but in this case it was true.

"Hi, Luckey."

"Hi, yourself." She'd pulled her gorgeous black hair back in a clip. Her emerald earrings matched the long-sleeved green blouse she was wearing with a black skirt.

She always looked so polished. It shook him all over again that if he hadn't taken this trafficking case, he would never have met her. The first chance he got, he would thank his brother for talking to him about the body he'd found on his beat.

"You realize you look like a world-class fashion model. Who would ever believe you're a college professor fluent in multiple languages?"

A smile broke out on her face. "Who would believe the day would come when I'd be helping a real Texas Ranger on a case?" He was coming to realize she had a hard time accepting a compliment. "Dad gave me the information you wanted. It's in this briefcase." She reached for it. "I'm ready."

They walked out to the car and Luckey held the door for her, then put the briefcase in the backseat. "I'll thank your father later. Have you eaten this morning?"

She nodded. "I just finished breakfast. What about you?"

"I'm good." He drove out to the main road and headed for Houston.

"Have you had any breaks in the case yet?"

He shot her a glance. "As a matter of fact I have.

I don't think I ever told you that Dr. Wolff found traces of some kind of topical painkiller cream on the sleeves of the victim's dress. It indicated that the person who dumped her body had the cream on his hands."

"That's an amazing find."

"Yeah, the doc loves his job. I asked the forensics expert at Ranger headquarters to identify the brand. Stan determined that it wasn't a cream manufactured here in the States, so I asked him to make some inquiries in Asia. And guess where he found it?"

Luckey felt her lavender-blue eyes fasten on him. "China?"

"No. Indonesia." He reached for her hand and squeezed it. "There's more. It's only sold through a mail-order business. Stan said that the cream is often used by athletes with sore joints. He also provided an important detail. He said that it causes a strong garlic odor in some men."

"Luckey!" Ally's cry resounded in the car's interior. "The young Chinese girl who wrote that message on her dress said the man smelled of garlic. That has to be the reason why she made reference to the Komodo dragon."

"Exactly. I'm convinced this guy operates here in Texas somewhere when he's not out of the country, kidnapping victims. I've got a call in to the pharmaceutical company in Jakarta. If they can't help me out with the guy's address, then we'll get a judge to issue a warrant and I'll go over the records of every shipment from Jakarta coming through the express mail carriers here in Texas. Eventually, I'll find a name and address."

"I *know* you will." The conviction in her voice was personally gratifying to him. "Whether he's Indonesian or Chinese, I bet he *is* blond. How many girls has he done this to? Wouldn't it be something if one of the young employees working at the orphanage had a terrible secret she didn't dare share? What if these girls could be helped!" Ally stirred in her seat and suddenly undid her seat belt. "I'm going to get the folder from my briefcase."

Before Luckey could pull off the freeway, she turned around and leaned over to get what she wanted. In the process, her flowery scent assailed him. Once she'd strapped herself back in, she opened a binder.

"Dad gave me this copy of the orphanage personnel records for you to keep. While you drive, I'll read every application out loud. They each have a photo. Anything that raises a red flag I'll pull for you... unless you'd rather do this on your own."

Ally, Ally, his heart whispered.

He gripped the steering wheel tighter. "When you get to know me better, you'll realize how much I enjoy your company, whether we're having fun or digging for answers."

By the time they reached Houston, he'd flagged one of the employees: Shan, the young Chinese woman he'd met. She was twenty, unmarried and had been working at the orphanage for the last six months. There were few details on her background. Luckey planned to investigate further when they got back to Austin.

Right now he'd worked up an appetite and drove them to the Chama Gaúcha Brazilian Steakhouse in Uptown, reputed for its great food. Hui's Silk Shop was located in the nearby shopping center, a place that exuded old-world charm for the upscale locals. Ally and he could walk there after their meal.

They walked into the restaurant and were shown to a table. The place was crowded, but he'd made a reservation. They ordered their food and Luckey applauded the quick service, considering they had to be at their appointment for one.

"Honestly, Luckey, these are the best pork ribs I've ever tasted," Ally exclaimed. "They've been dusted in Parmesan. I'll have to try this at home, but I bet it won't taste the same."

To his delight he was able to look at Ally all he wanted now that he wasn't driving. "Let's barbecue next week at my house and we'll experiment. You name the night—I know you have to be back on campus next week."

"I can't believe tomorrow is Sunday. This week has gone by way too fast."

"I was telling Persey earlier that I've been having so much fun, I've lost track of time."

A pretty flush stained her cheeks. "Me, too. Now I'll have to pay the price. I still have a ton of work to do before classes start."

He raised his eyebrows. "I'd be happy to help you,

but I don't read, write or understand Xiang or Mandarin."

She laughed. "I'm impressed you remember that much."

"I'm trying. Do you teach any language classes for beginners?"

"No."

"That's what I was afraid of."

"Why do you say that?"

"Because I'd sign up if you were the teacher."

"Luckey..."

"You think I'm kidding?"

"But you don't need to study Chinese."

"I think I do. It's a part of who you are. How about I spend evenings with you? While you do your work, I'll study and you can coach me on the side. I'm a quick learner. Then we'll have conversations while we go riding."

Her eyes deepened in color. "Be serious."

"Are you afraid you'll never get anything done if I'm with you all the time?"

"No!"

"How about I sign a contract? I won't touch you unless you ask me to."

"Don't be ridiculous."

"If that's not the problem, then what is?"

"You're a Ranger! You don't have that kind of time."

"I'm going to make time. If I can learn the basics of the language, it'll help me on this trafficking case. You learned the language, your father learned the language—so can I. Let's start tomorrow. You tell me what book to buy and I'll be over for a first lesson. I promise I won't bother you while you do your other work."

Ally shook her head. "You're impossible."

"That's what my mother says."

"I'll bet she does."

He sat back in his chair. "If you're not interested in seeing me again, all you have to do is say so and I'll leave you alone. The choice is yours. Think about it and let me know your decision when I drive you home later. Do you want anything else to eat?"

"No, I'm stuffed."

"Then let's go." Luckey paid for their meal with his credit card and escorted Ally from the restaurant. They walked across the street to the shopping center. He could tell her mind was working things out. She hadn't said no yet.

He was cautiously optimistic.

THINK ABOUT IT and let me know your decision when I drive you home later.

Luckey couldn't be serious, could he?

Ally was very aware of his rock-hard body next to hers as they made their way to the shop, and her mind filled with visions of the two of them doing homework together. It was ridiculous! They'd never get anything done, not when all she wanted was to be in his arms.

How about I sign a contract? I won't touch you unless you ask me to.

That would work for about two seconds, then—

"Here we are. Hui's Silks."

At the sound of Luckey's deep voice, Ally was jarred back to reality. They moved inside, where a lean, short, middle-aged Chinese man stood at the counter. He nodded to them.

"It's one o'clock. I appreciate punctuality. You're Mr. Davis, I presume. I'm Hui Guan."

"Mr. Guan? This is my friend, Dr. Duncan. We understand that we caught you before your return to Beijing. Thank you for taking the time to meet with us."

"Of course. What exactly can I do for you?"

Luckey pulled the pink dress sample from his pocket and put it on the counter. "Have you ever seen this material before? If you have, do you know where in China it was manufactured and where it could be purchased?"

"Is it Xiang embroidery?" Ally asked in Mandarin.

The man eyed her with interest before he picked up the fabric and studied it. After a moment he lifted his head and replied in Mandarin, "No. This is not made in the *shu zhi* method of the Hunan Province. Their weavers scour and bleach the longitude and latitude silks from cocoons first before weaving them. That way they no longer need more processing and can be used directly. No, this fabric is *shu* embroidery."

"Shu?" Ally repeated. Disappointment swamped her. She'd been so certain she was on the right track.

"See here. This is made with soft satins and colored threads because the raw materials are embroidered by hand. Regard the varied stitching method.

This lotus design is typical of the *shu* technique. It's unique and expensive."

"Do you know where it was made?"

"In Chengdu, the capital city of Sichuan Province."

"Do you have a shop in Chengdu?"

"No."

"Would you have a contact from the silk industry there that Mr. Davis and I could talk to?"

"I would have to check with one of my people in Beijing and get back to you."

"If you could do that, we'd be very grateful."

She turned to Luckey. "I'm sorry you couldn't follow the conversation." In a few words she told him what she'd found out.

Luckey pulled a business card from his breast pocket and handed it to the man. Mr. Guan did a double take. "You are a Texas Ranger?"

"That's right. I'm working on an important case. If it's possible, I'd like your contact to supply me with the name of every shop selling this embroidered silk."

"I don't know, but I will try."

"That's all I can ask. Before we leave your shop, is there anything you can tell me about this?" He reached into his pocket once more and drew out the other fabric sample.

Mr. Guan looked at it. "This lace brocade comes from Indonesia. Very expensive." Ally exchanged a glance with Luckey. This man was very good at what he did. "So many villages do their own kind of embroidery. You would need an expert."

"Could you put me in touch with one? I could send

that person a colored photograph of the swatch for identification."

"Again, I make no promises, but I'll see what I can do."

Luckey put the samples back in his pocket. "I appreciate your expertise more than you know. If you find out anything, call me day or night and reverse the charges."

Ally thanked him in Mandarin and they left the shop. Her mind was reeling with what she'd learned as they made their way to the car. When they stopped at a light on their way out of Houston, Luckey turned to her and searched her face. "What's going on in your mind that's made you so serious?"

"I thought I was on the right track when I assumed the pink fabric had been made in the Hunan Province, but I was wrong. It means…"

"It means you're thinking that the girl in the morgue isn't Yu Tan?" he said.

"Yes. I was a fool to imagine that a case like this could be solved so quickly."

The light changed and they turned to enter the freeway leading back to Austin. "I'm as disappointed as you are, Ally," he admitted, "but we've only gotten started. You've been to Chengdu to see the pandas, right?" She nodded. "Is it a long way from Changsha?"

"An hour and a half flight."

"You mentioned that your family went there with your friend's family every year. You *did* mean Soo-Lin's immediate family…"

"Yes."

"Did the women go shopping?"

"I'm sure they did. Soo-Lin and I went off on our own and met up with our families at the hotel at the end of the day." Ally stared out the window without seeing the landscape. "Don't you think it would be too big a stretch to suppose Soo-Lin's mother might have bought fabric there for Yu Tan's mother?"

"The day I became a Ranger, the captain told us that when you're hunting down a killer, nothing should be out of bounds in your imagination."

She smiled to herself. "When I told Dad you wanted to see the orphanage books, he said it appeared you were leaving no stone unturned in this investigation."

"My unorthodox methods continue to catch up with me."

"Unorthodox or not, he thought it was commendable."

"You made that up, but I'll take it."

Oh, Luckey... "I hope Mr. Guan will be able to get you the information you need."

"He seemed like a good man you can depend on."

You're the good man, Luckey. So good I can't believe I'm here with you right now.

"How come you and your wife didn't make it?" The question flew out of Ally's mouth before she could stop it. "I know what you told me, but there has to be more to it than the fact that you wanted to be a Ranger and she didn't like it."

Luckey took his time answering. "You're right.

I've had a lot of time to think about it. Truthfully, Linda needed me to plan my life around her even when we weren't together. Though she was the most important thing in my life—or I wouldn't have married her—I enjoyed my career. She resented those times when I had to be away, knowing she wasn't on my mind. I'm sure that sounds very harsh and selfish of me."

"Not at all. My father loved his career, too. Mom knew it and would have gone crazy if she didn't have her own life. Did Linda have a career when she married you?"

"No. She wanted to be a stay-at-home wife and mother like her own mom."

"Some women want that."

"I know, and that's fine. When we married, I worked hard to make enough money so she could stay home. I thought she was happy and we tried to have a baby right away, but it didn't happen. We talked to her OB and were checked out. He saw nothing medically wrong with either of us and told us to relax and give things time. But Linda just got more worked up as the months went by without her getting pregnant."

"Soo-Lin has been going through the same experience. I'm so sorry for you and your ex-wife."

"Twice in our marriage I had to be away when it was her fertile time. One night when I got home from a case, she made a demand. Either I give up law enforcement and find another career that didn't keep me away from her, or she was going to leave me."

"How painful for both of you."

"It was. I loved Linda, but she'd asked me to do something that I knew would turn me into a person I wouldn't like. In time she wouldn't have liked me, either. So we separated. I hoped she'd have a change of heart. We both wanted a miracle, but it wasn't meant to be and so we divorced."

Ally moaned inwardly. "Thank you for telling me."

He found her hand and threaded his fingers through hers. "I'm glad you asked. Now I want to know if you've made your decision about teaching me Chinese. I'm free tomorrow for my first lesson."

A laugh broke from her. "You said you'd give me until we got home."

"I'm an impatient man. Today you're discovering my many faults."

As far as Ally was concerned, he didn't have any. The explanation about his failed marriage had answered a lot of questions for her.

"All right. One lesson. Have you ever taken a foreign language class?"

"Three years of high school Spanish."

"How did you do?"

"You don't want to know." She smiled. "I wouldn't blame you if you think I can't do this," he added.

"I'm convinced you could do anything, Luckey. It's a question of how much time you have before your work prevents you from being able to keep it up."

"I won't know until I try."

Or until you've solved this case and grow bored with me. She didn't know if she had what it took to keep a man like Luckey Davis. All she knew was that she'd met an exceptional human being who blew every other guy she knew out of the water.

They reached Austin as the sun was setting. When he pulled up in front of Ally's parents' ranch, he said, "What would be the best time for me to come over tomorrow?"

Ally wished they didn't have to say good-night, but he hadn't suggested they do anything else. "Why don't we say four o' clock. That will give me time to finish my paperwork."

"That sounds perfect."

"I'll leave the briefcase with you and get it back later. Thank you for the wonderful lunch and the company. See you at four."

She opened the door and got out, knowing he probably had Ranger business to work on. After the revelation about his former wife, the last thing Ally wanted was to come off as being needy. She'd be seeing him tomorrow and that had to be enough for now.

AN EARLY SUNDAY morning phone call from Jakarta woke Luckey up. The man on the other end spoke passable English.

"Mr. Davis? My name is Rahmat Teguh, and I'm manager of Gema. I understand you called yesterday about a police matter. I've been instructed by the authorities to assist you."

"Thank you. I'm with the Texas Rangers in Austin, Texas. How long has your company been manufacturing DMSO cream?"

"Three years."

"I need the names and addresses of any people who've been ordering that cream over those three years from any location in Texas. This is a very urgent matter. When you can, please fax me that information and let me know which international express carriers were used. I'll give you the fax number." Luckey relayed the number slowly.

"I'll take care of it as soon as I can."

"Thank you very much."

Following that call, his mother phoned and told him the family was planning a barbecue for the next Saturday to celebrate his dad's birthday. Luckey promised he'd be there unless his latest case prevented him from making it. Once they hung up, he fixed breakfast before going out to the barn to exercise Persey. Riding his horse gave him time to think.

He couldn't expect TJ to get a warrant before Monday morning. As for Mr. Guan, he would need time to find a silk merchant from Chengdu who might be able to help Luckey. For the moment it was a waiting game.

Until he went to Ally's house, Luckey intended to research the personnel working for the International Junior Olympic Committee. He was intent on finding out what had happened to Yu Tan. Her disappearance had become personal to him. Someone on the committee could help him get in touch with gymnastic organizations within China that prepared young girls like Yu Tan to enter Olympic competition. If there was a tie-in to the murdered girl—who was also suspected to have been a gymnast—he wanted to find it.

Sundays were hard on Luckey because he couldn't conduct business as usual. For one thing, he wanted to get a surveillance team over to the orphanage to watch the comings and goings of Shan, the young Chinese woman he'd met who worked with the children. That would have to wait until tomorrow. If she was a trafficking victim, any testimony she could give would be helpful in hunting down predators like the ones dumping girls' bodies in the streets.

For another, he needed help from the passport office finding a person or persons who traveled between Texas and China and Indonesia on a regular basis over the last few years. But the official he needed to talk to, Mr. Jesse, wouldn't be available until tomorrow.

Luckey was glad when four o'clock finally approached. After a shower and shave, he dressed in jeans and a pullover before leaving the house to drive to the Duncan ranch. Ally came to the door wearing jeans and a pale yellow sweater that provided a stunning contrast to her black hair, which she'd left long today. Her eyes lit up. "*Ni hao*, Luckey."

That's right. She'd taught him that word at the orphanage. *"Ni hao."*

"Good."

"How do I say 'Doctor'?"

"I'm not a medical doctor. You can say *Laoshi hao*, which means 'Hello, teacher.' Let's do it again. *Ni hao*, Luckey."

"Laoshi hao."

Her smile widened. "Perfect. You've just had your first lesson in Mandarin Chinese. Come on into the dining room. We can work at the table." He supposed it was too much to ask that they get comfortable somewhere in the house on a couch.

When he'd come before, he'd noticed a Western motif dominated Ally's family home. She led him through a hallway lined with dozens of family pictures to the dining room, where twelve or more people could fit around the table easily. The large antique armoire had two Texas stars carved into the woodwork.

Ally saw where he was looking before she sat down at the head of the table. "When I was little, I used to pretend that those stars were Texas Ranger badges."

From a distance, that was exactly what they looked like. He grinned. "A precursor of things to come?" Luckey took the chair on her right. "It's a good thing for me you came back from China to fulfill your destiny. I'm eager to get started, but first I need to know how much you charge for lessons."

"Don't be ridiculous," she said. "Before we get started, would you like coffee or a soda? Maybe some tea?"

"Nothing right now, thank you. Don't I need a book or paper?"

"Not yet." The seductive curl of her lips intrigued him to no end. He couldn't go much longer without tasting them, but he'd promised not to touch her. "Mandarin is a tonal language. You need to master the tones. When you do that, we'll add new words. I've labeled these cards for you in order.

"Look at these first two cards. Both are labeled 1-1.

The left one shows an arrow indicating the direction of the sound of this Chinese word. The card on the right holds what's called a tone pair. Notice how the pair of words follows the graph on the left, with the arrow in the same direction and the same tone mark over the vowels."

Luckey studied both cards to get the drift. She made him pronounce the sounds several times.

"All right. Now I'll take the next two cards, labeled 1-2. This time notice that the arrow on this one goes in a different direction. Now look at the two words on the other card. They follow the arrow, and the tone marks are different. One is level, the other goes up."

"I get it."

"Good. There are four different tones. The fifth set of cards shows a dot to indicate that you will pronounce the word in a middle-toned voice, but we'll get to that later.

"Your first assignment will be to memorize these twenty tone pairs, since most Chinese words are made up of pairs. You must learn to pronounce them absolutely perfectly. I'll drill you until you can do them in your sleep. Then I'll teach you the writing."

He had news for her. His sleep was filled with dreams of her that had nothing to do with homework.

"They will form the basis for everything you learn. When you add a new word, you'll recognize which tone pair it matches and you'll be able to learn new words that much faster."

"You mean like memorizing your times tables?"

"Yes. Here are the next two cards, labeled 1-3. Notice the arrow is different again, as well as the direction of the slash over the vowel."

Learning Mandarin was a complete revelation to Luckey. By the time she'd taken him through twenty sets of cards, his head was spinning.

"In a few weeks you'll be able to tell me which tone pair matches a new word I give you. I'll send a disk home to help you with the meanings and pronunciation."

He looked up from the cards she'd handed him. "Are you saying our lesson is over? I've only been here an hour."

She laughed. "We can't do any more until you've had time to memorize the tones. Those cards are yours."

He put them in his pocket. "In that case let's go to my house and I'll barbecue us some hamburgers for dinner. It'll be my way to repay you for this lesson." He'd made certain he had all the ingredients on hand in case she said yes.

"I don't want repayment, but I won't say no to dinner."

Hallelujah. He got to his feet. "How early do you have to be at work in the morning?"

"Eight o'clock."

"Then let's leave now so we can enjoy a little time together before I have to bring you back."

She stood up. "I'll run upstairs to get that disk and meet you at your car."

"You didn't bring it down because you didn't think I would make it this far. Admit it."

Ally eyed him directly. "I didn't think any such thing. I simply forgot it. If you're fishing for compliments, I can tell you this much—I'm impressed you didn't throw the cards across the room and tell me you needed to leave because of some work-related thing you'd forgotten about."

"You'll never get rid of me that fast," he warned her.

They walked through the house to the foyer. After she hurried up the stairs, he went outside and leaned against his car while he waited for her. Before long she joined him. On their way into town, she flicked him a glance. "I've never asked where you live."

"Sunset Valley."

"It's not that far from here." She sounded pleasantly surprised.

"Which has turned out to be a nice perk for me, now that I'll be taking lessons from you on a daily basis."

Ally smiled and gave him a sideways look that said she didn't believe he'd last as a student of hers. "How long have you lived in Sunset Valley?" she asked.

"After the divorce, I bought a home there with property for my horse. But before I signed the papers, I drove the route to work. It only took me twelve minutes. That's what sold me."

A soft laugh escaped her lips. "You're as bad as I am. Before I applied for the position at the university, I timed the drive from the ranch. Only ten minutes. But I have to admit that depending on the kind of day I sometimes have, plus the evening traffic, it can seem like a hundred miles. Still, as much as I loved China, there's no place like home."

"I hear you."

Tonight he was taking her to his house. There was only one danger. He was so crazy about her, he might not let her leave.

Chapter Six

Ally was so excited to be going to Luckey's home, she was almost sick to her stomach. When they pulled into the driveway, the Santa Fe adobe house came as a surprise. Long beams extended outside the exterior walls in true pueblo style. She let out a little squeal. "Oh, my gosh, I love it!" His choice of home told her a lot about his taste and his idea of beauty.

"Come inside. I'll show you around."

The first thing she noticed when they walked through the door of the one-story home were the gorgeous handwoven Santa Fe style rugs scattered throughout the rooms. There were three bedrooms and a den. French doors from the dining room opened onto a charming patio. She loved the tiled kitchen, but her favorite space was the living room, with its floor-to-ceiling fireplace and little niches. The beams overhead added an authentic rustic feel.

"I love the curviness of this style."

"I'm glad you like it. If you want to freshen up in the guest bathroom, I'll go out to the patio and start the coals for the barbecue. After studying those tone pairs, I'm famished." She was already learning he didn't need an excuse to be hungry.

Seeing his home with the stamp of his personality on it had caused her to forget everything else. Ally pulled the disk from her purse and put it on the end table next to the couch. After washing her hands, she wandered out to the patio. She could see the barn and corral in the distance, but it was already beginning to get dark.

"If I were you, I'd never want to leave this place. You have everything right here."

"I do *now*." His eyes roamed over her, sending prickles of excitement through her body. "Let's go in the kitchen and whip up our dinner. I thought we'd have salad and lemonade iced tea with our burgers."

That sounded perfect. She followed him inside and pulled the salad ingredients from the fridge. He got out ground beef to form the burgers. "Be right back," he said when he'd made them.

Ally loved working with him. Before long they were able to sit down to a meal in the dining room. She could get used to this on a regular basis.

"How's Persey?"

"I took him for a run this morning. Tomorrow after work, why don't we pick up some Mexican food and bring Silver over here? We can go for a ride before you give me my second lesson."

She lifted her head. "Sounds great."

Luckey chuckled. "I'm trying my best to ensure I can see you again tomorrow. But if you'd prefer

Italian, we can do that, too. What time do you think you'll be leaving the university?"

"Around three, if I'm lucky."

"Will it be pushing you too much if I come by at four with the trailer?"

She wanted that more than he could possibly imagine. "Tell you what. Since neither of us knows what our day is going to be like tomorrow, I'll phone you when I'm ready to leave my office. If something comes up that prevents either of us from getting together, we can make arrangements for the day after."

Luckey nodded. "As long as we're arranging our schedules, it's my dad's birthday on Saturday. How would you like to go to Dripping Springs with me? The whole family will be there to celebrate. We can take the horses."

He wanted her to meet his family? Nothing could have made her happier. "I'd like that very much."

Luckey sat back in the chair. "You've just made my day. Much as I'd like us to go in the living room and watch a movie, I know you have to get back home."

"I happen to know you have a full agenda tomorrow, and it probably starts earlier than my day. I'll help you with the dishes," she said, and got up to clear the table. He grabbed what she didn't and they took everything to the kitchen.

After refusing her help with washing the dishes, Luckey walked her out to his car. On the drive home she remembered to tell him she'd left the disk on the end table in the living room.

"I can't wait to get started," he told her.

She shot him a glance. "You sound about as excited as I am to face my students tomorrow."

"Since we've met, I count the hours when I'm not with you."

"It's been a wonderful week," she conceded. Ally could relate like mad. "Luckey? Would it be against the rules for you to tell me how the case is going so far?"

He reached over to squeeze her hand, as he'd done the other day. "As soon as I have any solid information, you'll be the first to hear."

"Okay."

"That's not a put off. It's too early in the investigation."

"I realize that."

"I'm hoping for results soon." Luckey kissed her palm before letting her hand go. The touch of his lips sent a tremor through her body. She wanted more, but there'd be no physical relationship unless she let him know she wanted it. Luckey had so far proved that he was an honorable man who wouldn't go back on his word.

You're the one who went along with the boundaries he set, she reminded herself. So why was she upset? The question plagued her for the remainder of the short drive back to the ranch. In danger of begging him to kiss her, she reached for the door handle the second he drew up in front.

He turned to her. "Thanks for the lesson. You're an excellent teacher. *Wanan*, Ally."

She blinked. "You've learned the word *good-night*! You even said it perfectly."

"I looked it up earlier today on the internet and practiced the sound."

"I'm impressed."

"I hope to keep impressing you."

"You already have," she answered in a tremulous voice, before getting out of the car. "*Wanan*, Luckey." When she locked the front door of the house behind her, she was out of breath.

"Ally?" Her mom appeared in the foyer. "What's wrong?"

Nothing was wrong. *Everything was wrong.* She wanted this case to be over so they could be together on a normal man-and-woman level, with no other issues involved.

"Honey?" Beatrice prompted. "Where have you been?"

"I gave Luckey a lesson in Mandarin, and then he invited me to his home in Sunset Valley for dinner."

"A lesson?"

"Yes. He says he wants to learn Chinese. It will help him when dealing with the Asian trafficking cases."

Her mother raised her eyebrows. "Well, that's a terrific excuse for spending time with you."

"I like being with him," Ally confessed, "but…"

"But what?"

"He's been married before."

"Does he have children?"

"No. He was divorced eight years ago. It's the reason they divorced that has me worried."

"Why?"

"I don't want to be a reminder of her."

"How could you do that?"

"She didn't want him to be in law enforcement, because it kept him away from her too much. She asked him to change his career, but he couldn't do it."

"Of course he couldn't. The woman who falls in love with a Texas Ranger will never change him," her mother said, with conviction based on experience. "But you don't want to change him. So what's wrong?"

"I'm crazy about him!" she cried, revealing her frustration. "I just don't want him to know how much I care…in case he feels suffocated and backs away, like he did with her."

"Who suggested the Chinese lessons?"

"He did."

"Well, you must be doing something right or he wouldn't be setting himself up for heartbreak a second time."

"What do you mean?"

"Maybe he's got a deep-seated fear that you'll retreat because of his job, so he's taking lessons for insurance."

Was that the real reason? Her mother had given her a lot to think about.

"Where's Dad?"

"He's gone up to bed."

"That's where I'm headed. I've got to be at the university by eight." They climbed the stairs together. "Thanks for the talk."

"Anytime, honey," her mom said, and they gave each other a quick hug.

Ally went to her room to get ready for bed. Once she got under the covers, it was impossible to turn off her mind. Luckey didn't seem like a man who was afraid of anything, but who knew his demons after suffering through a divorce? If she held him off for too long because of her fear that he'd lose interest, would she do damage to their growing relationship? That question haunted her until she finally fell asleep.

LUCKEY WOKE UP early Monday morning with Ally on his mind. Because they'd made tentative plans for the evening, he was able to channel his energy and get busy. First, he arranged for a team to sit outside the orphanage for the next week and track Shan's comings and goings. He sent the guys her photograph and the necessary information to identify her.

Next, he made inquiries with the Junior Olympic Committee and was put in touch with an official who'd been on the committee for central China's most recent Youth Olympic Games in Nanjang. Luckey wanted the names and contact numbers of Olympic coaches for the Chinese contestants from the Beijing region and Hunan Province.

If he could talk to several of them, he might find out where the younger girls trained, in cities such as Yongzhou. Perhaps one of those centers would yield a record on Yu Tan and he could learn more about her and the names of the instructors. It was worth a shot. The official promised to send him information as soon as he could.

An impatient Luckey hung up. The information from Indonesia hadn't been faxed yet and there had been no word from Mr. Guan. Luckey decided to call the passport office.

"Mr. Jesse? I'm glad I've got you on the line. This is Ranger Davis from Company H headquarters in Austin, Texas. I need your help on a new case. It's a priority for me."

"Aren't they all?" the man teased. "Go ahead."

Luckey explained the nature of the crimes he was investigating. "I need names for the last three years, those who've used Texas as a port of entry at any time."

"Give me an hour and I'll email you the information."

"Thank you. I'll be waiting for it."

With a little time left on his hands, he grabbed the index cards Ally had made for him and took a ride on Persey while he studied. He needed the disk to hear the proper way to make the sounds, but could memorize the meanings of the tone pairs. His poor horse had to listen to him try to pronounce them.

He patted his palomino's neck. "Don't worry. I haven't lost my mind yet." After his ride, he put Persey back in the barn. "If all goes well, we'll go riding tonight with Ally and Silver."

When he sat back down at his computer, he found

a file from Mr. Jesse in his in-box. Yep, he had his work cut out for the better part of the day.

After making a list of the individuals, Luckey ran names through the Integrated Automated Finger-printed Identification System criminal database that brought up photos, too. He needed to find out how many had aliases and/or warrants out on them. He checked his watch while he waited for the results: 2:40 p.m.

It didn't take long for the computer to give him the information he'd requested. Of the two hundred fifty names, a hundred and fifty had been arrested on different charges or were dead. Seventy had outstanding warrants on them from virtually every state in the union. Thirty were convicted felons, but had still managed to get a passport by using a different name and fake passport. They were still at large.

At three thirty his phone rang. He checked the caller ID and clicked on. "Ally?"

"Hi! Sorry I'm phoning later than I intended to. Our department is going into an unscheduled meeting because of some new policies. I probably can't be home before six thirty, so I'm afraid we're going to have to postpone our ride at your house. But if you want to come over at seven, we can have another lesson. That is if you're free."

"I'll bring dinner. See you at seven."

Luckey had three hours before he needed to shower and pick up the food. That gave him enough time to start plowing through the list. He didn't know exactly what he was looking for, but if something jumped out at him, he'd flag it.

One by one he studied the profiles and accompanying mug shots with last known addresses picked out from their original passport photos. They would be of vital importance when he went through the records at various express mail carriers.

Out of the first hundred, he flagged three criminals who'd managed to escape the no fly rule. Jason White, from Indiana, was wanted for the brutal slayings of two upper management executives in a Chicago software company. "He speaks fluent Mandarin and has a master's degree in international business. He's an avid golfer, snowboarder, skier, dirt biker and has been a soccer player. White enjoys being the center of attention. He's been seen at several local Shanghai nightclubs as well as international soccer matches with various girlfriends. His known aliases are: Jacob White, John Jacob, Jaron White, Jim Jacobs, RJ White. He has ties to Illinois and Alaska. He's probably in possession of a Glock 9 mm and a .45 caliber handgun."

Then there was Enrique Santoya, an American born Puerto Rican from Florida, a ship's mechanic for the Meersman Shipping Container Company traveling to various ports in China and Indonesia from Los Angeles. "Speaks passable Mandarin and Indonesian. Served five years of a forty-year sentence in Folsom Prison, California, for kidnapping and murder of three female illegals before his escape. Known to box and work out in gyms. Aliases are: Rico Santos,

Eric Santana, Santo Ricardo. Favorite Chinese weapons are a Cold Steel Dragonfly O Tanto knife and a Columbia River Hisshou knife."

Luckey also flagged Winn Klein from Oregon, a former figure skater and tennis player. "Wanted for murdering his two Chinese wives, both athletes he met in China and brought to Seattle. His mode for killing was suffocation. Could be working in a restaurant in San Francisco's or Houston's Chinatown. Had a porn site. Speaks Mandarin. Hangs out in sports bars or may be working in one. His aliases are: Wyn Klene, Kley Winn, Kelly Wyn, Win Klien, Wynn Kleen."

Any one of the three criminals could be involved in human trafficking here in Austin, where they stayed under the radar. Luckey needed to get through the other fifty names, but this was a start. He glanced at his watch and realized he'd have to hurry to get to Ally's house on time. After calling ahead for Mexican food, he got ready, grabbed his index cards and raced out of the house.

When he pulled up to the ranch, he met her father walking around the front in his cowboy boots. "Mr. Duncan." The two men smiled and shook hands. "I want to thank you for the information from the orphanage."

"You're welcome, but please call me Larry. To be honest, I would never have thought of looking into the staff's backgrounds, but it makes perfect sense."

"I've got a surveillance team set up in case any of

the workers could be in a bad situation. I'll know in a few days if we find anything."

Mr. Duncan's eyes went to the sack Luckey was holding. "Something smells good. Don't let me keep you."

"You're welcome to eat with us."

"Thanks, but Ally's mother and I have already had dinner. I still have work to do out here. Go on inside. I'm sure my daughter's waiting."

Chapter Seven

Luckey climbed the front steps and had started to ring the bell when the door opened. "I thought I heard voices out here. *Ni hao*, Luckey."

"Laoshi hao."

With a feeling of déjà vu, he followed Ally into the dining room. She was a vision, as usual, in khaki pants and a white blouse that tied at the side of the waist. She'd done her hair in a loose knot. How her students were able to concentrate when looking at her was beyond him.

"Did you get those tiny orange earrings in China?" he asked her.

"Yes. They make the most delicate enamel jewelry."

"I like them. In fact, I like all your jewelry," Luckey said. "I like the way you dress, think, act, eat, smile, walk, ride, look, smell, feel."

Ally's cheeks turned pink and she smiled. "Thanks," she said, looking at the floor and then raising her eyes to meet his again. "How was your day?"

"Like climbing a mountain. I couldn't decide where to start my ascent."

She chuckled. "I bet you've blazed half a dozen trails up that mountain."

"You're close. How did things go at the university?"

"My day was long and busy. You have no idea how much I've been looking forward to this evening. This smells fantastic."

"I'm hungry myself."

He reached inside the sack and put their containers of enchiladas and black beans with rice on the table. She'd set it with place mats and sodas. With the addition of a container of chips and salsa, they were all set. "Mexican is one of my favorite foods," Luckey told her.

"I think it's everyone's."

"Just so you know up front, I didn't have time to listen to the disk yet, but I've been memorizing the meanings of the tone pairs."

She ate a chip. "How did you manage to do that while climbing a mountain?"

"On top of Persey."

Ally broke into laughter. "Better be careful or you'll turn your palomino into a new version of Mister Ed, the talking horse who spouts Mandarin. I saw a rerun of that old television series a while back. It had some ridiculous episodes."

They both ate with relish. "The nice thing about a horse is that it doesn't talk back. It just listens. Persey is very patient with me, especially when I'm frustrated over a case."

Her smile deepened. "If my horse could talk, what tales she would have to tell. Silver knows all my secrets. Imagine what those two would have to say if they could speak to each other."

"Who says they don't have a secret language? Nüshu Texas-style for equine lovers only."

"Hilarious!"

"He let me know he wants me to bring Silver over ASAP."

An impish look crept into her eyes. "Maybe they *do* communicate. When I went out to the barn a little while ago, my horse wanted to know when Persey was coming again."

"You can tell her it will be as soon as my *laoshi* wants me to drop by for my next lesson. Maybe if I impress her enough tonight, she'll take pity on me and invite me over again tomorrow evening."

Luckey could hear Ally's mind working. "Tuesdays and Thursdays I have a lighter schedule. Tomorrow, depending on your workload, we could plan to ride around four, then come back to eat and study."

It was music to his ears. "In that case, let's get started on my homework."

While she cleared the table, he cleaned up the cartons and put everything back in the sack. Once that was done, he pulled the cards out of his pocket and handed them to her. "Go ahead and ask me anything you want."

She looked down. Let's start with the word *easy*."

"Rong yi."

"Next time."

"Ming yian."

"Thanks."

"Xie xie."

"What."

"Shen me."

"China."

"Zhong guo."

Ally went through all twenty pairs before handing the cards back to him with shock written on her face. "You have one of those photographic minds. I can't believe you've memorized those perfectly since last night."

"But I haven't pronounced them right."

"Can I expect that you'll be able to say them flawlessly tomorrow during our ride?"

"I'll try."

"Luckey—I'm kidding. I don't know anyone who learned all the pairs as fast as you have. You're amazing!"

"I'm motivated." Especially when she looked at him the way she was doing now.

"I'm speechless, to be honest. Let's go through each card and I'll work on the pronunciation with you."

For the next half hour she got him to mimic each sound until she was satisfied. "You have a gift," she said, once they'd gone through all of them.

He put the cards in his pocket and sat back in his chair. "Let's list yours, shall we?"

"I mean it." The blue of her eyes deepened. "I lived

in China fifteen years. It took me a long time to master what you've already done. I'm not at all surprised you're a Texas Ranger. It's almost scary how fast your brain takes in a concept, pulls it apart, figures it out and builds on it."

"You make me sound like a machine, but I assure you I'm not." After a pause he said, "Do you still have work to do tonight?"

"Yes. I wish I didn't."

He believed she meant it. "So do I." Time to leave. Luckey got up from the table. Her parents were around. "Better not see me to the door."

Her head reared back. "Why?"

Luckey sucked in his breath. "Do you really have to ask?" He wheeled around and walked out of the house to his car. If she'd followed him to the door, the promise he'd made not to touch her would have gone up in smoke.

Tomorrow night he'd tell her he couldn't abide by it any longer.

ALLY WAITED TOO long to chase after him. By the time she reached the door, he'd gone. The sensual tension between them had reached flash point. Aching with need, she realized she couldn't do this anymore.

After turning out the light, she hurried up the stairs to her room. Her cell phone was in her purse. She pulled it out and sat on the side of her bed to call him. It rang three times. *Please answer, Luckey.*

On the fifth ring she heard the click. "Ally?" *Thank heaven.* "Is something wrong?"

"I—I didn't want you to leave." Her voice faltered. "Surely you know that."

"It was better I did."

"If it's all right, I'll bring Silver over to your house tomorrow after work. I'll supply the food and we'll talk." They couldn't be alone at her house.

"I'd like that very much, but answer me a question. What are you afraid of?"

She gripped the phone tighter. "Of making a mistake with you."

"In what way?"

"I've never been married, but *you* have."

"Go on."

Ally shivered. "It would be the most normal thing in the world for you to see traits in me you don't like that remind you of your ex-wife." Her voice shook. "Sorry. That didn't come out right. I know you loved her and I didn't mean any disrespect. I just keep putting my foot in it. I guess what I meant to say is, I'm trying to be careful with you."

"That works both ways, Ally. Since you're unlike any woman I've ever known, the possibility of comparing you to anyone else doesn't exist."

"But there's one truth we can't escape from. I *am* a woman."

He let out a bark of laughter. "Yes, you are, and I'm a man. How do you expect me to respond to that?"

"I don't know. I feel like a fool."

"We'll figure it out tomorrow when you come over. Call me when you leave the university, to give me a heads-up."

"Okay. Good night, Luckey."

She didn't know if she could last that long. Ally knew for sure she wanted to throw out the rules she'd imposed. All she could think about was getting in his arms.

ALLY'S PHONE CALL had given Luckey his first real indication that she felt the same way about him that he felt about her. Tonight she'd been the one to reach out to him on a purely personal level. She had initiated tomorrow evening's meeting and wanted it to be at his house, where they could be alone.

Overjoyed by this much progress, he drove home feeling a kind of euphoria he'd never experienced before. Ally was the real deal. He couldn't believe she'd been living here in Austin since summer, right under his nose. He'd flown over her parents' ranch while he'd been working another case.

Never would he have dreamed she lived there. They didn't live that far apart from each other. Luckey was getting the feeling it was all meant to be. He didn't want to think anything else.

After he got home he put the disk in the computer and stretched out on the couch in his den to practice the tone pairs. Ally had gone over the pronunciation with him tonight. The sounds were easier to understand now. He marveled over the knowledge she'd acquired. Because of it, he'd been able to delve deep into this murder case.

After half an hour had passed, he removed the disk

and checked his email one more time. Nothing of any consequence showed up on the screen. Before he went to bed, Luckey looked through the remaining names from the criminal database. He scrolled halfway before he found another possible suspect.

"Robert D. Martin, known to hold a US and Chinese passport, is sought for the armed robbery of eight million dollars from a security company in Las Vegas. He took two security employees hostage at gunpoint, handcuffed them and injected them with a poison, killing them. Fled to China and is still at large. Fluent in Xiang. Has awards in kung fu and gymnastics. Aliases are: Dino Morten, Bobo Marten, Sid Marteen, Momo Demott, Angelo Martin. Carries a .32 caliber pistol."

Luckey read the rap sheet.

Caucasian with red hair, but the passport listed him with black hair. What was his real hair color?

Age forty. Fluent in Xiang. Why?

A gymnast. When and where? Why did he come through Texas?

A poison to disable his victims. Did they eventually die?

It wasn't until Luckey went to bed that he remembered something Stan had said about DMSO.

The cream acted like a nonsteroidal anti-inflammatory and was used by athletes trying to cut down on joint pain. It could also be poisonous if injected in gross amounts.

Was it possible that Robert Martin used DMSO and that it was also his brand of poison?

FIRST THING THE next morning, Luckey got on the phone to the Las Vegas police. He wanted to know the facts in the security robbery case involving Robert D. Martin, and asked to speak to the detective who'd investigated it. Like always, he had to wait for the man to call him back.

After feeding Persey and taking him out to the corral, he hurried back inside for a phone conference with TJ. Luckey learned that the judge had issued the warrant. That was the news he'd been waiting for. He gathered up the folder with the sheets of names and took off for headquarters to pick the warrant up.

CY STOPPED HIM in the hallway. "I wondered when you'd show up. Come on in and talk to me."

"You're just the man I wanted to see," Luckey said, following him into his office and perching on the edge of his desk.

"The guys are waiting to hear how things are going with you know who."

Luckey smiled. "They're getting better and better, but I've got some murders to solve."

"I know what that's like. I was in the middle of Kellie's case when I fell headlong in love with her. What can I do to help speed things along?"

"You mean it?"

"I offered, didn't I? TJ hasn't assigned me a new case yet."

"Then come with me and I'll give you the lowdown on the way. Give me a minute to pick up the warrant."

A short time later, the two men got into Luckey's

car. He handed his friend the folder. "Go ahead and read over the four rap sheets. I'm hoping an alias of one of these felons will match up with a name on a carrier's records as someone who received a package from Indonesia. To make a connection would mean solving the case."

"And getting on with the important stuff in life," Cy added.

"I can't wait for that," Luckey mumbled.

"Then let's make it happen!"

Together they did the rounds of three international express carriers and obtained copies of the available information. Then they returned to headquarters and sequestered themselves in Luckey's office to begin hunting for a match.

Cy shook his head. "No matter how many times I go over a rap sheet, I'm stunned to see how much evil exists out there."

"Tell me about it."

While they worked, Cy took a phone call on his cell. After he hung up he said, "TJ wants to talk to me. I'll be back."

"I'm not holding my breath. I've got a feeling you might be getting a new case. Thanks for the help."

"You've done the same thing for me before. Keep us all posted, hear?"

"Will do, Cy. Thanks again."

Cy's leaving reminded Luckey the day was getting away from him. They hadn't found a match yet. He gathered up everything he'd been working on and left the office for home. He wanted to take a quick shower and shave before Ally came over.

She phoned while he was on his way home and said she'd be at his house in forty-five minutes with Silver.

"I'm holding you to it, otherwise I'll come looking for you," Luckey said, grinning. "You're pretty important to me, you know."

"Then you know how *I* feel," she replied.

Ally...

Chapter Eight

When Ally pulled up at Luckey's place, he was already outside, leaning against the corral. She drove her dad's truck along the side of the house to the barn and made a turn in front of it before stopping. His truck and trailer were parked farther on.

He straightened and walked toward her with purpose in every step. She could hardly breathe as he opened the truck door and pulled her into his arms. They closed around her body, not allowing her feet to touch the ground.

"I thought you'd never get here," he whispered into her hair. "If I don't kiss you right now, I'm not going to make it."

"I want you to kiss me," she confessed, inching her lips over his smooth jaw to the compelling mouth she'd longed to taste. Ally wanted him in such an elemental way, there was no thought of holding back. His hunger matched hers as their mouths met in a fiery explosion of need she had no way of controlling.

Ally hadn't been with a man for several years, but nothing had prepared her for this. Luckey was taking her to a place she'd never been before. His kiss was a conduit to something much bigger, igniting her passion. All sense of time and place fled from her mind while she devoured him and was devoured in return.

His hands roamed over her back, pressing her to his well-honed physique. She had no idea when he'd lowered her so her feet touched the ground. The two of them moved and breathed as one person. No air separated them in their struggle to get as close as possible and not let this ecstatic moment end.

He bit her earlobe gently. "You've set me on fire, Ally," he whispered. His breathing sounded ragged. "I could do this for the rest of my life and never come up for air." Once again his kiss engulfed her, robbing her of words, of breath. She'd been rendered witless and it was all his doing.

As the minutes went by, the heat built between them. Ally trembled against his hard-muscled body, loving everything he was doing to her, loving the way he made her feel. "You've done something terrible to me, Luckey."

"*How* terrible?" He stole another deep kiss from her mouth.

"Can't you tell? I've never felt this way in my life."

"You think *I* have? You've turned me into someone I don't know anymore. But as much as I want to steal you away and make love to you nonstop, we'd have to marry first. Anything less would never satisfy me."

Ally swayed in place and looked into his eyes. "You want to marry me?"

"I know I've shocked you, but there it is. That's

the way I feel about you. But I'm sure you need time to think about marrying a man you've only known… what is it? Ten days?"

"Luckey…" She couldn't take it all in.

His hands slid to her hot cheeks. "I didn't expect to meet someone like you. You've come as a total surprise to me when I least expected it. After we ran into each other at your office, my life changed and will never be the same again." He kissed her lips once more. "Come on. Let's saddle our horses and go for a ride while I still have the ability to let you out of my arms. Persey's in the barn waiting for us."

Ally couldn't move. Her Texas Ranger had just made her happy beyond measure. Riding was the last thing on her mind. As she slid her hands up his chest to let him know much she loved him, his cell phone rang.

The sound jarred her so badly she moaned in protest, but knew he had to answer it.

He pulled it from his pocket and checked the caller ID. "This is Davis." Ally clung to him and waited. She felt his body stiffen. "I'll be right there," he stated, his voice grating. This sounded serious.

No…

Just like that her joy turned to pain. She almost begged him not to go, but stopped herself in time. He wouldn't leave her if it wasn't an emergency. She knew that.

Don't let him see what this is costing you, Ally.

She put on a smile and lifted her head. "I know you're needed. Call me tomorrow." Ally raised up on tiptoe to kiss his lips before turning to get back in the truck.

He followed and shut the door for her. His troubled, dark brown eyes searched hers for understanding. "I'm sorry, Ally."

As much as she knew he didn't want to go, she could already tell his mind was elsewhere. "It's your job," she said through the open window. "I understand."

"I'll phone you later tonight if I can."

"Don't worry about it."

"This is the last thing I expected to happen." He leaned through the opening and kissed her fiercely before hurrying down the drive to his own car, parked in front of the house. Ally trailed him out to the main road before he waved to her, and they went in different directions. By the time she reached the ranch, she realized she'd just experienced what it had been like to be his ex-wife.

She eyed their uneaten picnic in the sack next to her.

Her body ached with unassuaged longings that wouldn't go away until she was in his arms again.

There was no guarantee of when she'd next see him.

And if he'd been called in to a dangerous situation, he could be injured. Or worse...

Ally poured out her thoughts to Silver as she put the horse back in her stall for the night. The more she thought about it, the more she marveled that his ex-wife had stayed with him for as long as she had.

To realize that every time he walked out the door she might never see him again was anathema.

That will be your life if you marry him, Ally.

He hadn't asked her for an answer yet. He was giving her time to think about it. Luckey had told her why his first marriage hadn't worked. He'd given her a taste of love without trying to make love to her. If he had, she would have gone wherever he led, because she loved him with every fiber of her being. He was honorable to the core.

By the time she went inside the house, she'd lost her appetite and went up to her room to do some work before she left for the university in the morning. Her parents had gone over to her uncle's house, sparing her from having to explain why she'd come home early with red eyes and a blotchy face.

Ally still hadn't heard from Luckey before she turned out the light and went to bed. It wasn't until the next morning on her way to work that she heard some news on the car radio that turned her inside out.

"We have breaking news that Michael Landrey, a Texas Ranger with Company H in Austin, Texas, was shot in the line of duty in the Highland Park area last night, leaving two wanted criminals dead. A veteran with the department, the many-times-decorated Ranger died at the hospital in the early hours of the morning. He was coming up on retirement and leaves behind a wife and two married children. More information will be forthcoming on our noon broadcast."

Ally was so badly shaken, she sat in her reserved parking space at the university in order to pull herself together. The news explained Luckey's silence. She'd been around him and his friends just long enough to realize these men had a rare bond with each other. The loss of one of their own would leave its mark.

Tears poured down her cheeks. That poor man's family. His wife's pain had to be excruciating. After thinking he'd be home with her to enjoy the years they had left together, he was gone.

One of Ally's colleagues pulled into the space next to her. Embarrassed to be seen in her condition, she wiped her eyes and hurried inside to her office. One of her students was waiting there to talk to her.

Functioning on autopilot, she was thankful when they concluded, and was about to make her way to her classroom when a tall, striking male appeared in her doorway. Her heart thumped outrageously.

"Luckey…" She wanted to launch herself into his arms, but couldn't do that with other students and faculty walking back and forth. He was dressed in the same clothes he'd worn last evening. It meant he hadn't been to bed yet. His attractive features looked drawn with pain. "Come in," she said. "I heard the news on the radio."

He closed the door behind him and took her into an embrace. "I've been up all night and need to go home to sleep, but I had to see you first. I promise to call you tonight." He kissed her softly on the lips before disappearing out the door.

Ally clutched one of the chairs nearest her. While she stood there trying to catch her breath, she heard a voice. "Dr. Duncan? Can I talk to you for a minute about my thesis?"

AT A QUARTER to seven in the evening, Luckey heard his cell phone ring. Roused out of a deep sleep, he reached for the device on his bedside table. It was Randy. The tragedy had hit both brothers hard, because Mike Landrey had been a colleague of Randy's as well as a personal friend of their father's.

The sight of his grieving widow and family at the hospital had come as a double blow to Luckey, considering he'd just told Ally he wanted to marry her. He might have known Mike's death would be blasted over the news, but he'd hoped to be the one to tell her first.

This was the kind of news that had always terrified Linda. She'd feared that one day a couple Rangers would come to their door and she'd know why. Luckey had no doubt that when his ex-wife heard today's news, she'd be thankful she'd moved on.

But all his concern was concentrated on Ally. What had the news done to her? When he'd found her at her office that morning, all it took was one glance at her face and he knew he'd arrived too late. They needed to talk.

Wearing a pair of sweats, he walked through the house to the den, intending to check his emails before phoning her. No sooner had he sat down at his desk then his cell rang again. It was Phil from the surveillance team.

"Phil? What's up?"

"I've just sent you some videos. When we posted ourselves down the street from the orphanage on Monday, we saw a man in a black car parked across the way. The young woman in question came out the front door at 5:00 p.m. and got in the car. We followed it to a spa downtown off Windsor Road."

Luckey *knew* it. He'd had a feeling about the young Chinese woman, who couldn't meet his eyes and had suspicious bruising.

"The car turned into an alley regulated by a gate," Phil continued. "Our video shows men coming and going from the spa all night. Tuesday morning the same man in the black car came out through the gate and drove the woman to the orphanage, at 8:00 a.m."

"Could you tell his ethnicity?"

"No, but I'm sure forensics will figure it out. The guys who replaced us got a video of her being dropped off and going inside the orphanage the next morning. After the car drove off, another black car with a different driver pulled up across from the orphanage and stayed until the young woman came out again at five. Obviously she is under a constant watch."

Luckey whistled. "Her 'handler' is making a ton of money off her and won't let her out of his sight, even during her legitimate day job. Did the routine change at all?"

"No. She was driven to the same spa after work. This morning they got video of her being driven to the orphanage again at eight. Sid and I took over and got video of her leaving at five and getting back in the car. We followed it downtown to the same spa. We're still here. How long would you like us to keep this up?"

"I've got everything I need. Great work! I'll take it from here."

Halfway through the videos Phil had sent, Luckey stopped watching and phoned Ally.

"I'm so glad you called." She sounded anxious.

"I'd like to come over, if it's all right with you."

"What are you thinking?"

"I think I can't wait to see you. I'll be there soon."

He showered and dressed as fast as he could. Before leaving the house, he put the videos on a flash drive and took it with him. En route to the Duncan ranch, he phoned Art, the teenager next door who took care of Persey when Luckey couldn't. He asked him to walk his horse around and make sure he had food and water.

With that taken care of, he pulled up in front of Ally's house and raced to the porch. She stood in front of the door waiting for him, looking beautiful in a soft blue sweater and jeans.

He crushed her in his arms and kissed her long and hard. "I needed this tonight." One kiss grew into another as their mouths communicated, until he lost complete track of time.

"Thank heaven it wasn't you shot in the line of duty," she said at last.

His lips brushed over her delectable features. "I don't want to talk about that tonight, Ally."

"Then we won't. Did you get some sleep?"

"Enough. How was your day?"

"Normal."

"I need to solve this case ASAP so I can have a normal life with you."

"Does that mean you have to leave again tonight?"

"I never want to leave, but there's been a development I'd like to discuss with your parents. Are they here?"

She nodded. "Does this have something to do with the orphanage?"

"Yes."

"Can't you tell me?"

Luckey took a quick breath. "I thought I'd explain everything to the three of you at the same time. The surveillance team I sent to watch the orphanage has emailed me some videos I want you to see. They're on a flash drive."

She grasped his arms in alarm. "Are you saying Shan is involved?"

"That's right. I saw signs when I met her."

"What signs?"

"Bruising on her arms. She wouldn't look me in the eye. There's a manner these victims portray that reveals they live in fear. I felt then she was a victim."

"Oh, Luckey…that's so horrible."

He drew Ally close, rocking her back and forth. "We can do something for her, but we have to proceed with great caution, and your father needs to be on board if we're going to ask for her help."

"Let's go in the family room. While you put the flash drive in the computer, I'll ask Mom and Dad to join us."

Ally started for the door, but Luckey pulled her back. "Not until I have more of this." He found her mouth and kissed her until they were both swaying.

"Later we're going to have a long talk about the rest of our lives. How does that sound?"

"I—I agree we need to talk." Her voice faltered. He didn't know if he liked her response, but she'd turned to open the door. Luckey followed her inside to their family room. "Go ahead and set things up. I'll get my parents."

Within a few minutes the four of them had congregated around the computer screen. After a warm greeting from her parents, Luckey inserted the flash drive. "Just watch everything, then we'll talk."

The videos were self-explanatory. When they were finished, he glanced at Ally, who looked horrified. Her mother and father eyed each other in silence. Luckey removed the flash drive.

"As you can see, this woman is caught without hope. It's my opinion she's doing extra work at the orphanage to make more money for the man who owns her. Not all victims have another avenue for money. No doubt she was brought into the spa with the promise of work. The going salary is usually $30,000. But they can never buy themselves out of the contract they sign.

"She could provide us with a lot of information if we handle this carefully. How did she get here? Where is she from? Does she have family? Who did this to her? I don't know that she would be able to shed any light on the murders, but maybe she knows someone at the spa who could give us crucial information. Naturally, we'll free her and relocate her to a safe life without causing any notoriety to the orphanage."

Ally's father got to his feet. "How will you get information from her?"

"One of the men at the bureau who speaks Mandarin will go undercover at the spa to procure her services. He'll get her alone and tell her we're going to free her from her situation, but we'd like information. After she's safe, we'll learn all we can from her and raid the place. The whole ring will be arrested and we'll free the other women they've kept in bondage."

"Do it, Luckey!" Ally's mother cried. "I'm devastated for Shan, who has to work under such ghastly circumstances before coming to work at the orphanage every day. She's such a lovely girl and so sweet with the children. All these women need to be freed."

Larry nodded. "Nothing would make us happier. Anything we can do to help, just let us know."

"You already have, by giving me a copy of the orphanage records."

"Thank you for what you've done and are prepared to do, Luckey," Ally's father said sincerely. "I know you'll keep us informed. Come on, Bea."

Luckey watched them exit the den, leaving him alone with the woman he loved. She sat on the edge of the couch with her hands clasped. "We have to talk, Luckey."

"I know you're anxious to hear the details about Mike's death."

"Only if you want to tell me." She got to her feet. "But that's not what's on my mind. I've been thinking about Shan. If another Ranger could get rid of the man waiting outside the orphanage tomorrow, I'd drive over and convince her to come to the ranch with me. If you were here waiting, you could ask her all the questions you want and I'd provide the translation."

He shook his head, but she kept on talking. "The proof she'll provide will enable you to arrest those evil men and close down the spa. You've got videos. With the women freed, you'll probably be able to gather a lot of information needed to make inroads in the trafficking situation here in Texas. You know it's a perfect plan. You need me to do this." Her lavender eyes were begging him.

"I refuse to let you sacrifice yourself like that," he said through gritted teeth.

"I lived under scrutiny of the MSS authorities for fifteen years. My whole family did. What if I want to do this for all these girls? I'll ask my teaching assistant to cover my classes tomorrow. Think about it. Shan doesn't trust any man, but she knows and trusts me. We've become friends. When I tell her what's going on, she'll do as I say."

Damn if Ally wasn't making perfect sense.

"IF ONE OF your undercover officers approaches her at the spa, she'll be too suspicious and it won't go well. It could put another Ranger in needless danger. I've always wanted to help. Now's my chance to get involved. You *have* to use me, Luckey. To quote you, the sooner the better. While you think about it, I'm going to get the sandwiches I made for us. I'll only be a minute."

The second she left the room, Luckey phoned TJ and ran the whole thing by him.

"What in the hell tipped you off about the Chinese girl at the orphanage?" After Luckey told him why he'd gone there in the first place, his boss asked, "Do you see any holes in Dr. Duncan's idea?"

"In all honesty, no, but as we're both well aware, the best-laid plans can go wrong."

"Do her parents know?"

"Not yet. They'd have to be told."

"I doubt they'll go along with it."

Luckey closed his eyes tightly. "Probably not."

"You don't think the man driving the Chinese woman back and forth is tailed by a backup?"

"That was the first thing I asked the guys to watch for. They saw no signs."

"You know what, Davis? You have such scary instincts, all I can say is I'm glad you're on our side." Luckey smiled to himself. "However you want to handle it, go ahead, and round up the help you need. Vic is between cases. I'll ask him to get things in place for the victims to go into protective custody. Get that spa closed down and there's another citation waiting for you."

Luckey heard the click as Ally came into the den with a tray of sandwiches and clam chowder. "What would you like to drink?"

"Do you have coffee?"

"I can hear a long night behind that request. Be right back."

Nothing escaped Ally. She returned fast and they settled down in front of the coffee table to eat.

"Thanks for this. I didn't eat after I woke up today."

"That's what I thought." Her eyes searched his as she bit into a roast beef sandwich. "So what's it going to be? Do I call my assistant or not?"

Ally, Ally... He ate a whole sandwich before he said, "You'd have to tell your parents first."

"I already did, when I went to the kitchen. Mom's all for it. Dad doesn't like it, but he knows I'd do it anyway, so he gave me his blessing, as long as I follow your instructions to the letter."

"You're so incredible." Luckey finished the chowder and took a drink of his coffee. "That was delicious, by the way."

Her anxious gaze played over him. "Next you're going to say you hate to eat and run, but there it is."

Luckey leaned closer and kissed her. "I don't want to leave you, but if we're going to put this plan in action, I have to start things moving. Don't get up, Ally. I'll see myself out and call you within two hours." He reached for the flash drive and hurried out of the house to his car.

On the way to his house, he phoned Vic. "Luckey Davis," his friend said when he picked up. "TJ just informed me you need help on your case. I'm your man."

"Now I know my plan is going to work. I'll need you first thing in the morning. Let me explain what's going on…"

ALLY SAT OUTSIDE the ranch house in her car Thursday morning and waited for Luckey's call, adrenaline pumping through her body. The phone rang at 8:20 a.m. She picked up. "Luckey?"

"Go ahead and drive to the orphanage. Shan was dropped off on cue. Her handler has been arrested thanks to Vic. Park where you usually do, along the side. You're being followed by one of the crew, so don't be alarmed. I'll know your progress every step of the way. Be careful."

"You, too, Luckey."

"Always. I'll see you and Shan at your house."

Ally hung up and headed for the orphanage. In case she had to persuade Shan, she'd brought the six sheets of paper with the Nüshu writing in her purse. Before getting out of the car, she said a prayer that this was going to work.

There were always three workers on duty at any given time, plus the cook and her assistant. One of them answered the doorbell to let her in. She talked with everyone like she usually did, until she found Shan in one of the bedrooms helping two of the children get dressed.

The bruises on her arms should have been noticeable before, but Ally hadn't been looking. Now she saw that there were bruises on her legs, as well. Shan had been beaten. Who knew how many times?

Ally played with the children and helped Shan accompany them to the kitchen for their breakfast. "While they're eating," she said, "I'd like to talk to you, Shan. Let's go back to the bedroom."

The young woman nodded and followed her. Ally shut the door and sank down on one of the twin beds. She motioned for Shan to sit on the one across from her.

"Shan? Can you read the Nüshu language?"

She blinked. "No."

"But you know about it."

"Yes. A secret language."

"That's right. I have an example of it in my purse." Ally pulled out the papers and showed them to her. "I'm going to translate what these words say. They were written in blood on the cheongsam of a dead Chinese girl found in Austin two weeks ago."

Shan listened while Ally read the words the young woman had written. With each sentence, tears filled Shan's eyes, until they ran down her cheeks and she bowed her head.

"You're one of the many young women who have been kidnapped and brought to this country. The police have videos of the man who has enslaved you, bringing you to work and taking you back to the spa every night. If you'll come with me right now, I'll take you to my house, where the man you saw me with last week will talk to you.

"He's a Texas Ranger and will take you and the other young women to safety, where you'll never have to worry again. My father will arrange for another helper to replace you here. By tonight the spa will be closed down and the men involved put in prison. It's your choice if you want freedom. I'm going out to my car. I'll wait fifteen minutes, then I'll be gone. I'm here to help you, but you have to want it."

Ally sent up more prayers as she left the orphanage and walked out to her car. She didn't know what was going to happen. Shan had to be frightened out of her mind.

After fifteen minutes had passed Ally decided the young woman wasn't going to come. She started the car, but as she put it in gear, Shan came running out of the house. She opened the door and got into the front seat.

Ally squeezed her hand. "You're very brave, Shan. In ten minutes you're going to be free."

Knowing that her handler had been taken care of by the Rangers, she backed out of the driveway and they took off for the ranch. Behind her she could see the car tailing her, and fought tears to think Shan was one of the lucky few who was able to escape. There were years—probably a lifetime—of rehabilitation ahead of her, but she would now be able to live her own life. Depending on where she'd been kidnapped in China, maybe she could return and be united with her loved ones. Maybe not.

When Ally saw Luckey standing on the porch with her parents, her heart jumped into her throat. She hadn't seen his vehicle. Someone from the bureau must have driven him over. "You're safe now, Shan. Let us take care of you."

The three of them moved toward the car. Ally's mom drew Shan out and put her arms around her.

Speaking to her in Chinese, she walked her up the steps into the house.

Her father hugged Ally hard. "My brave girl. Thank God you're safe."

"Shan's the brave one."

Over his shoulder her gaze fused with Luckey's. After her father let her go and went into the house, Luckey enveloped her in his arms. "You're a sight for sore eyes," he murmured.

"It worked!" she cried softly.

He kissed her face and hair. "How did you convince her so fast?"

"I showed her the secret writing and translated what was written. That got to her."

"You're brilliant and wonderful and so many things, I don't know where to begin." For a minute the world stood still as his mouth closed over hers and they attempted to express their feelings for each other. Ally groaned when at last he pulled away from her. "We're going to spend all Saturday together," he whispered against her lips. "But until then I'll be wrapped up in business."

"I know that's what you have to do."

"A crew of special agents will be coming to get Shan in a minute, but I'd like to learn what I can from her before they arrive."

Ally met his lips one more time in an explosive response of need. She couldn't bear to let him go, but she had to. He eased her away, but kept hold of her hand as they walked inside the house. The others were in the living room. Ally took a seat on the couch next to Shan and her mother. Luckey found a chair near her father, opposite them.

Beatrice reached in front of Shan to grasp Ally's hand. "We've found out Shan lived in Loudi."

Ally's gaze shot to Luckey. "That's only about a hundred miles from Changsha."

"Ask her to tell you what happened."

Once Shan had finished explaining in Mandarin, Ally translated what the young woman had revealed. "Her parents ran a flower shop and lived above it with her younger brother. She was seventeen when someone grabbed her from behind while she was leaving her gymnastics class after school."

Luckey's jaw hardened. "She's from Hunan Province, too, and is a gymnast. Her story sounds like what happened to Yu Tan."

"That's what I'm thinking. All Shan remembers is that when she woke up, it was in a horrible place where men used her and she couldn't get away. She was moved around for a long time. One Chinese man told her he would take her to America and get her a good job, but she'd have to pay him back by working. If she didn't cooperate, he'd hurt her brother.

"He showed her a picture of him, so she knew the threat was real and signed the contract. She doesn't know where the man moved her. She was never left alone for a second. The next thing she knew, another man was in charge of her here and told her she had to work at the orphanage to earn extra money. But he kept her wages. She tried to run away, but he beat her."

Luckey leaned forward. "Ask her for a description of the man who first kidnapped her."

Ally did his bidding. Shan shook her head and muttered a string of words Ally translated. "She only remembers he had funny hair."

"What does that mean?"

"That he wasn't Chinese, but he spoke Xiang."

Funny hair? Could she have meant blond? The analogy to the Komodo dragon's split yellow tongue, written in the secret language, flashed through Luckey's mind. With Shan's revelation, certain information he'd gathered was beginning to come together. "Ask her if she associated any kind of smell with him. This is very important."

Another conversation ensued. Shan nodded. Ally looked at him. "She said he smelled like the grumpy old farmer who supplied leeks for one of the markets on their street in Loudi."

Leeks. A white vegetable like onions and...garlic.

Luckey got excited over the details she'd provided. "What about the man who's been handling her here in Austin?"

Ally got an answer from her. "He's Chinese."

"Does he speak Xiang, too?"

The answer came back. "No. Mandarin."

Just then the front door bell rang. Luckey hurried to answer it and, as expected, found a female agent from the trafficking division who spoke Chinese there. He accompanied her inside and introduced her to Shan before turning to Ally. "Tell Shan I'm going to headquarters with her and Agent Chen, where we'll make her comfortable. After she's been processed, you can all visit her."

Ally quickly conveyed his words to Shan, who got up from the couch. She hugged her before they all walked to the front door.

In an aside to Ally, Luckey said, "I'll phone you as soon as I can about Saturday."

She nodded, but it killed her to see him go. "Make it soon."

Once they were gone, she turned to her parents. "I need to get to the university. When I come home later we'll talk."

No doubt they were dismayed by her swift departure, but Ally needed to keep busy or she'd go crazy, until she could be with Luckey again.

Chapter Nine

By late afternoon, Luckey and Agent Chen had talked to all but one of the fifteen female victims who'd been brought into the security housing area for debriefing. Their conversations had been recorded and would be printed out for the files.

He'd heard a different story from each one as far as where they'd come from and their individual circumstances. But one thing remained constant: they'd been kidnapped in their mid to late teens and locked up like animals. They were told nothing and had no hope of escape. He couldn't wait to go to the jail and interrogate the men who'd been arrested. But he had one more victim to visit.

A different female agent met him at the door. "This girl is from Jakarta, Indonesia."

Luckey's pulse picked up speed. They went inside. He told the agent what questions he wanted her to ask the girl. Soon he got an answer that solidified the theory he'd been forming.

"She said the man who first kidnapped her was

waiting for her when she was the last one off their school bus to attend a gymnastics meet."

"Can she describe the man?"

The agent translated his question, then told him, "She says he smelled like a pigsty."

"Has she been around pigsties?"

"She says her grandfather was a pig farmer. Their family had to help deworm the animals with garlic and wormwood."

Luckey reared his head back. "Ask her to tell us anything else she remembers about her kidnapper."

The response came in a minute. "He spoke Indonesian, but he was big like a lot of American men."

"Does she mean fat?"

Another question. Another answer. "No. He had a tall, muscular build."

"Did she see his face?"

More conversation Luckey couldn't understand. "No, just his hair."

"What color was it?"

He waited for the answer. "Like the brass sculptures on the church."

Bingo!

Her captor had to be the head of this particular trafficking ring. All Luckey had to do now was find him and nail him.

"I know who I'm looking for," he announced, elated, when he saw Vic coming out of TJ's office a half hour later. "How did the raid go?"

Vic's black eyes flashed. "Your plan to arrest the man out in the car for stalking worked like magic and opened up the worst can of worms you ever saw. The spa has been shut down and the men arrested. They're still being interrogated."

"No one's given up the name of the mastermind yet?"

"They will. I just got out of a meeting with the boss to let him know what's been happening. He's wanted to clean up that area of downtown for years. This is a big win for the department, thanks to you."

No. It was thanks to Ally. "I couldn't have done this without your help, Vic. There'll be more wins when we catch this fork-tongued dragon."

His friend squinted at him. "Forked tongue? Is that a secret code or something?"

"A secret code from a secret language. Come down to my office while I check my emails and I'll explain. First, though, I need to call Ally."

"While you do that I'll get us some coffee and doughnuts."

Luckey sank down in his chair and phoned her.

She answered on the second ring. "I was hoping it was you!"

"Where are you, Ally?"

"I just got home from the university. What's happening?"

"The spa has been closed down and the men arrested. But the big news is I've identified the guy responsible for this trafficking ring. I'm positive he's the one who kidnapped the victim in the morgue. Ally, it's looking more and more like she may be Yu Tan."

"Oh, Luckey…"

"There's more. He also kidnapped Shan and one of the other girls we picked up at the spa. She's Indonesian. I just came back from talking to her. With the information I got from the three women, I have the description I need to go after this pervert."

"Were we right when we thought the victim at the morgue had written an important clue?"

"Absolutely, and she provided more than one. We're now looking for a tall, muscular American with brass-colored hair, who speaks Indonesian, Xiang and Mandarin, smells of garlic and holds awards in gymnastics and kung fu. I'm going to get him, Ally. Give me until Saturday, then I'm all yours. I'll call you tomorrow night to arrange a definite time to come and pick you up."

"I'll be ready."

"Take care. You're the most important person in my life."

As he hung up, Vic walked into the office with the coffee and doughnuts. He darted Luckey a meaningful glance. "Guess I don't need to ask how things are going between you two. Jeremy wants you to bring Ally over to the house. She has received my son's seal of approval."

"She's got mine, too, Vic. All I have to do is solve this case so I can concentrate on the two of us."

"I hear you."

"Take a look at these rap sheets. After what I know now, I think the last one is the ringleader."

Vic walked around the desk and studied them. He read the last one aloud.

"'Robert D. Martin, known to hold a US and Chinese passport, is sought for the armed robbery of eight million dollars from a security company in Las Vegas. He took two security employees hostage at gunpoint, handcuffed them and injected them with a poison, killing them. Fled to China and is still at large. Fluent in Xiang. Has awards in kung fu and gymnastics. Aliases are: Dino Morten, Bobo Marten, Sid Marteen, Momo Demott, Angelo Martin. Carries a .32 caliber pistol.'"

Vic lifted his head. "I think you're right about this one."

"Cy helped me compare these rap sheets to the list of names we got from the express mail services. I feel in my bones this has to be the guy, but I haven't tied his name to any aliases yet." Luckey told him about the Komodo dragon analogy and the residue of DMSO on the sleeve of the victim.

His friend's black brows lifted. "You figured all that out from the secret writing?"

"With Ally's help."

"Maybe she's in the wrong field of work."

"If Dr. Duncan had been anywhere except at her office that day, we would never have met. I don't even want to think about it."

"What more can I do to help? Use me before the boss calls me in on another case."

"You pulled off today's sting with your usual finesse. I'll never be able to repay you. Now go on home and be with your family. Tonight I'll be making phone calls here and overseas, trying to zero in on this guy."

"You're sure?"

"Positive."

"If something comes up and you need me, I'm only a call away."

Luckey knew that. He watched his friend walk out the door before he started scrolling through his latest emails. Good! The one from Las Vegas had come through. He opened it and called the phone number given to him by the police department for a Lieutenant Hayes.

"Hayes speaking."

"Lieutenant? This is Ranger Davis from Austin, Texas. You're the one who investigated the case involving Robert Martin?"

"No. That was Lieutenant Torelli. He passed away a year ago." Luckey frowned. "But I've looked up the file on Robert Martin for you and can see he's still at large," Hayes continued. "Do you want me to send you a copy?"

"Please. He's responsible for a human trafficking ring out of China. I need to find him ASAP."

"I'll send it now."

"Thank you very much."

"Anything to help."

Once he'd received the file compiled by Lieutenant Hayes, Luckey read through it carefully. Several pieces of news leaped out at him. Martin was the adopted son of a Caucasian mother, Anna Martin, a gymnast from Freeport, Texas, and a Chinese father,

Sima Wang, who was a sports facilitator from Beijing. Through Wang, Martin had a Chinese passport.
The family had traveled back and forth to mainland
China, and then one day none of them were heard
from again. Years later the news broke that after
committing the robbery and deaths of the guards by
DMSO injections in Las Vegas, Nevada, Martin had
evaded arrest. It was presumed he'd fled to China
under one of his many aliases.

Luckey was puzzled. Who were the birth parents?
Why was the child given the adoptive mother's last
name? What happened to the adoptive mother and father? It didn't sound like an ordinary adoption. Something was fishy from the get-go.

Tired and hungry, he left the office for home.
After a visit to the barn, he made himself a meal and
worked until late. He wrote down two addresses from
the UPS carrier that had delivered cream to Freeport,
the town Robert Martin's adoptive mother was from,
neither of them Martin's aliases. The answers Luckey
sought about the recipients and Martin's birth parents
would have to wait until morning, when he planned
to drive there and investigate.

In his gut he knew another clue was hiding that
would bring him closer to capturing the sick man
who'd destroyed so many lives. Luckey finally fell
asleep with the knowledge that Saturday was coming
and he'd soon be taking Ally home to meet his family.

ALLY DIDN'T KNOW you could love a whole family on
sight, but after meeting the forty people gathered for

Luckey's father's birthday in Dripping Springs, she sure felt as if she did.

Everyone was so nice and laid-back. Randy was more reserved, like his father, and had his darker hair. Luckey took a little more after his dark blonde mother, Melanie, who was outgoing and the sweetest, warmest person Ally had ever met. The woman had a charm she'd passed on to her son.

Everyone congregated around Luckey, especially Randy's kids and the children of his cousins, as he showed Ally the ranch on horseback. The whole family rode together and it was obvious they all loved their Texas Ranger, but she was way of ahead of them in that department.

A stream ran through a portion of their property. When their group reached an oasis-like area shaded by a grove of oak trees near the creek, they dismounted. A fabulous spread had been prepared ahead of time, with tables and chairs for everyone. Between three-legged and gunnysack races, with prizes for the winners, Ally had never laughed so hard or had so much fun.

Gifts appeared for the patriarch of the Davis family. To her surprise, Luckey gave his father a scarf exactly like the one she'd given Jeremy. "You're now an honorary Ranger, Dad," he told him.

She'd bought his father a black domino mask. Luckey's shock was visible when his father opened her package. He put the mask on and tied the ends at the side of his head.

Randy grinned. "Good grief, Dad. You look like

the real thing! Do you know something we don't? Is retirement already too hard on you?"

Everyone laughed. Luckey's hand slid to Ally's where they sat.

"No, no, no," their mother called out. "Your father's days for saving the world are over. We're going on a long cruise."

Randy's wife, Robin, shook her head. "He'll never last, Mom. Give him one day on board and he'll want to get off at the nearest port and head back to Texas."

More laughter ensued. "She said a mouthful," Luckey whispered to Ally. He rubbed her palm with his thumb. "Are you ready to take a ride with me? Alone?"

Her heart turned over. "You think your family will let us slip away?"

"Just watch." He got up from the table. "I hate to have to do this, but I've received a message that means I have to get back to Austin."

There was a collective protest.

"I love you all. Happy Birthday again, Dad."

Ally followed Luckey as he walked over to his parents. They both got up and all four of them hugged. Ally eyed the older pair. "Thank you so much for this wonderful day," she said.

Luckey's father smiled. "Come on over anytime, Ally. You'll always be welcome."

Luckey's mother walked her over to her horse. "I've never seen my son so happy. Whatever you're doing, I'm very grateful."

The wistful note in her voice caused Ally to swallow hard. "You've raised a wonderful son. I wish we could stay and help you clean up, but—"

Melanie shook her head. "If the day ever comes when Luckey actually stays for a whole party and is the last one to leave, I won't believe it. I married a restless man and I've gotten used to it."

Ally had the suspicion his mother was telling her that Luckey was restless, too. But Ally had already learned that about him. His mom had to know why Luckey and his wife had divorced. Was Melanie afraid Ally wouldn't be able to handle it? Was this her way of warning her?

"Ally?" Luckey had come up behind her. "It's time to get going."

"Thanks again," she whispered to his mother, and mounted Silver. Luckey got on Persey and they started back to the house. She darted him a covert glance. "Did you really have to leave the party?"

"Yes. I want time alone with you."

She took a risk. "You mean before you have to leave me in a little while?"

The answer was a long time in coming. "Yes. What did my mother tell you?"

Ally smiled to herself. "Something I already knew. I like your family a lot."

"You'd blush if I told you what everyone thinks about you, but you have a hard time accepting a compliment, so I won't."

"Am I that bad?"

"Worse." They rode in silence for a bit.

"Have you learned anything more about the case?"

"I did when I went to Freeport yesterday, but before I tell you about that, are you ready to talk about how you felt when you heard Ranger Landrey had been killed?"

That was the subject they'd been avoiding until now. She took a deep breath. "You already know."

"It wouldn't help to tell you a tragedy like that rarely occurs?"

"No. I wish it did."

"Would that be the biggest reason you wouldn't want to marry me? Or do you have other reservations? Did Mom tell you I'm hard to live with?"

"She said you were restless like your father, but that she'd adapted."

"She adapted to a lot of things, but it's a lie that she didn't worry about him getting killed. She worried every time he left for work, but she put up a good front around him. Robin's the same way around Randy, but he and I know differently."

"That describes my mother, too," Ally confessed. "Dad will never know how hard her life with him has been at times. He's had death threats. It's a miracle he wasn't shot during his tenure.

"They never spoke about the close calls and Mom and I pretended we didn't worry. But nothing could have been further from the truth. Early on, she decided to fight her fear by doing something dangerous herself. That gave me courage and I helped her. Somehow we survived those years."

A grimace marred Luckey's handsome features. "Only to meet me and hear me bring up marriage on the same night one of our legendary Rangers was gunned down."

Ally bit her lip. "I won't lie. It shook me to the core. I thought of his poor wife. I thought of your ex-wife. I'm sure when she heard the news, she was thankful she didn't have to bury you."

"I have no doubt that's true. I hate to tarnish your vision of your childhood idol, Ally, but it has to be said."

She shivered at the direction their conversation was taking. "What do you mean?"

"The Lone Ranger didn't marry. Now you know why. It's good we cleared the air. Come on. Persey and I will race you to the trailer."

He took off like a silver bullet. She let him go. Of course she couldn't catch up with him, but that wasn't the reason she didn't try. Their conversation had reminded him of his divorce and the choice he'd made to stay with the Rangers, which meant losing his wife.

By the time she reached his horse trailer, the shadows of evening were lengthening and she knew he wouldn't ask her to marry him a second time.

Silence reigned on their way back to her parents' house. When he pulled up in front of the barn, he darted a glance at her and said, "I've decided to get a tutor for my Chinese lessons. Agent Chen said she'd fit me into her schedule when she could. She could never be you, but we can't always have the things we want."

He didn't say it in a cruel, punishing way. Luckey

simply sounded resigned, but every word caused Ally excruciating pain.

After levering himself from the truck, he walked around to help Silver back out of the trailer. Ally took over and led her horse into the barn. While Luckey stood by, she fed and watered her Morgan before walking out of the barn.

Gathering her courage, she looked up at him. "I had a fantastic time with your family. Thank you for that. I know you need to get back to work. You don't have to drive me to the front of the house. I'd actually prefer to walk."

His face had turned into a frozen mask. "As I dig further into this case, I'll give you and your parents updates. You know where to find me if there's anything you need. I think you're an amazing woman, Ally Duncan. What you did for Shan won't be forgotten. It's been my privilege to spend time with you." He tipped his Stetson and climbed into his truck.

Her vision blurred as he drove off. She felt as though she'd been run over by a tank and couldn't move.

WITH PERSEY PUT to bed, Luckey grabbed a beer out of the fridge and stood in the kitchen, feeling at the lowest ebb of his life. Nothing could alter what had just happened between him and Ally. If he lost her, he didn't know how he was going to carry on.

He was in hell, but he had a job to do. Work would help stave off the red-hot pain until he dropped from sheer exhaustion.

Yesterday he'd spent all day in Freeport, three hours from Austin, looking for evidence of any kind that would lead him to find Robert Martin. The two addresses where cream had been delivered turned out to be a health care facility and an elderly couple's home.

As for the adoption, he'd discovered it had been closed. That was too suspicious under the circumstances. Luckey visited Brazosport Independent School District in Freeport to make inquiries about Anna Martin. No one could shed any light on her.

He'd decided to visit some kung fu facilities. At the fifth one, an older man in charge of a Chinese gym that taught martial arts told him Anna Martin had worked out there for several years. She'd won some local awards for kung fu. He remembered that she took take care of her sister's boy. When her Chinese boyfriend wanted her to go to China, she wouldn't go unless he took the boy, too. They'd had a big fight, and the manager of the gym never saw them again.

Luckey was excited to have learned that Robert Martin was the son of Anna's sister. It brought him a step closer to solving this case. The adoption had to be illegal. Luckey went to the vital statistics bureau, where he found a birth certificate for a Caucasian baby boy, Robert, the son of Sybil Martin and Andrew Mott.

Further inquiry proved the two parents were deceased.

Momo Demott was one of Robert's aliases. Sid Marteen was a close fit for Sybil. That led Luckey to look up any Martins, Marteens, Motts or Demotts, who'd lived in Freeport, but nothing that could be linked to Robert Martin turned up. No matter. Luckey wouldn't stop until he found him and sent him to prison for the rest of his life.

At two in the morning Luckey finally staggered to bed. As soon as he woke up the next morning, he went outside to see to Persey's needs and put him in the corral. After eating breakfast, he started cross-checking all Robert Martin's aliases against the remainder of names he hadn't yet gone through from the international carriers' files.

He left his phone on voice mail while he worked. Randy called to announce his approval of Ally. Following that call, he heard from both his parents and three cousins, all letting him know they were very impressed with her. The only person he knew who wouldn't call him was Ally herself. But when he looked for her name on his phone anyway, and discovered it wasn't there, he received another gut punch that came close to incapacitating him.

Around noon an email came through from Mr. Guan. At last! Luckey opened it.

I have two contacts for you, Mr. Davis. A silk merchant in Chengdu named Mr. Li Wang will be expecting to hear from you. Also a Mr. Mahyadi Suharto from Jakarta. Their phone numbers and email addresses are written below. I hope this helps you in your investigation.

Luckey was impressed with Mr. Guan. He replied to the email to thank him for his invaluable help. Then he sent messages to both men, explaining the situation so they'd understand this was a matter of life and death. Thirty minutes went by before Mr. Wang responded by email.

Mr. Davis, we've analyzed the fabric sample photograph. The particular pink silk you've inquired about is a relatively new product manufactured eighteen months ago here in Chengdu. Our company has sixty outlets throughout China. Seven are in Chengdu. It would be most helpful if you could supply a date for the time you believe the pink and-gold embroidered silk would have been purchased and in what city and province.

Where and when? At this point Luckey was really stretching the boundaries of his imagination to think Yu Tan's mother had been in possession of that fabric. But Beatrice Duncan *had* traveled to Chengdu with Soo-Lin's parents. Was it possible she'd made a purchase for the Tan family? There was only one way to find out. If nothing jived, he could forget that route to discovering the name of the girl in the morgue.

He phoned Ally, steeling himself not to react when she answered. To his surprise, he got her voice mail. He left a message that he was coming over, but on a Sunday she could be anywhere. Without hesitation he reached for the silk sample and left the house for the Duncan ranch. Maybe she was at home, maybe not. But no matter. He needed to talk to her parents and would make this an official visit.

Beatrice answered the door. "Oh—Luckey—I don't believe Ally knew you were coming. She's out riding."

So she *was* home. "It's all right. I'm here on official business, but I did leave a message with her. Is your husband home?"

"Yes."

"I'd like to talk to you for a few minutes if that's possible."

"Of course. Come in."

She led him to the living room and went to look for him. In a minute they'd joined Luckey and sat down. He explained why he'd come. "My contact has traced the fabric found on the girl's body to Chengdu, where it was manufactured.

"Ally tells me you've been home from China since the end of August. Is there any chance you visited Chengdu anytime in the last eighteen months?" Before they had a chance to respond, Luckey frowned. "Wait, now that I think about it, Ally said you always went to see the pandas in the fall, which would put you there prior to eighteen months ago. That discounts my theory."

"No," Larry interrupted. "Our very last visit to Chengdu was in June."

Beatrice nodded. "That's right!"

"I had to attend a US-China bilateral meeting on commerce and trade, and took the family with me. We invited Soo-Lin's family to go with us. Soo-Lin came with her husband."

Luckey's heart began to pound. "Where did you stay?"

"The Saint Regis Hotel."

He leaned forward. "Beatrice, this is very important. Did you go shopping while you were there?"

She nodded. "We shopped our heads off for the whole two days."

"Do you remember visiting a fabric shop with Soo-Lin's mother?"

"I know we went in and out of several stores. Their silks are beautiful beyond belief."

Luckey pulled the fabric sample out of his pocket. "I'd like you to take a good look at this." He handed it to her.

She took it from him and examined it. "Larry? Turn on the lamp." He did her bidding so she could get a better look at it. "That gold thread with the pink silk... I *do* remember it. Soo-Lin's mother bought it and two other fabrics from that shop to take home as gifts for the extended family."

Beatrice turned to him. "Oh, Luckey—I can't believe it, but I'm sure you've found Yu Tan! You don't know what this will mean to their family. Thank you! Thank you!" She threw her arms around his neck and wept.

Elated to realize his wild hunch had paid off, he was slow to realize Ally had just walked into the living room. "What's happened?" she cried, looking agonized, but so beautiful, even wearing jeans and a pullover, that he could hardly breathe.

Her dad put his arm around her. "Luckey has just learned that Yu Tan is the girl in the morgue."

"What?" Her face had gone white.

Luckey nodded. "Your mom took one look at this sample and remembered the day last June when she and Soo-Lin's mother bought fabric at one of the shops in Chengdu. Soo-Lin's mother wanted to give them as gifts to her extended family."

"That means Mr. Guan contacted you." Ally sounded as if she was in shock.

"He's already performed one miracle for us and he's also put me in touch with a silk merchant in Jakarta. If that lead pans out, we might be able to identify the Indonesian girl in the morgue, too. I believe taking you with me to Houston to act as interpreter was the charm. I'm indebted to you for that, Ally."

Luckey turned to her father. "Let me know how you would like to handle giving the news to the Tan family. We'll go from there and make arrangements for Yu Tan's body to be shipped back home."

Larry walked over to shake his hand. "You've closed down that spa, freed Shan from a life of horror and now you're about to give a daughter back to her family. There's no way to repay you for what you've done. If there's anything *our* family can do for you…" His voice shook.

"It's my job, Larry, and couldn't possibly compare to the one you did for our country over the last fifteen years. But as my boss would tell me, my job's not done. I've still got to find the leader of that trafficking ring and am getting closer, thanks to Ally. She was the one who could read the secret message on Yu Tan's dress that gave us the clues we needed. But your daughter's brilliance couldn't be news to you."

"Luckey…" Ally whispered.

"We are now looking for Robert D. Martin, a tall, dark blond Caucasian gymnast operating under many aliases, known to dye his hair black and red. He has both an American and Chinese passport and speaks Xiang and Mandarin.

"I went to Freeport and discovered that Robert's adoptive mother, a local expert in kung fu, raised Robert, her sister's son, and married a Chinese sports facilitator from Beijing. Both of them have disappeared off the radar. I went to the vital statistics bureau and found a birth certificate for a baby boy, Robert, the son of Sybil Martin and Andrew Mott. Both are now deceased.

"Momo Demott is one of Robert's aliases. Sid Marteen is a close fit for Sybil. I looked up any Martins, Marteens, Motts or Demotts who'd lived in Freeport, but nothing that could be linked to Robert Martin turned up. No matter, I only have a few more addresses to check in one section of Austin. I won't stop until I've found him and sent him to prison for the rest of his life. As soon as I can prove this cream was delivered to him, we'll have positive proof that Robert kidnapped Yu Tan, Shan and an Indonesian girl who was freed from the spa. Who knows how many hundreds more throughout China."

He heard gasps from the three of them.

"All his victims are young gymnasts. He disappeared after robbing a security company in Las Vegas of eight million dollars. He killed the guards with an injection of DMSO. He himself uses the DMSO cream himself for joint pain, which was found on the sleeve of Yu Tan's cheongsam. Robert Martin is dangerous and still on the loose, but we're going to catch him. I believe he's operating in Houston or Austin when he's here in the country.

"Please forgive me, but I need to get back to work, so we'll talk again later." He reached for the sample lying on the coffee table and strode from the room without looking at Ally. He couldn't. It hurt too much.

Chapter Ten

Ally watched Luckey disappear, taking her heart with him.

"There goes an exceptional man," her father murmured. His remark brought her head around. "Why don't you tell your mom and me what's going on? We don't know you like this."

She couldn't hold it in any longer. "A few days ago Luckey asked me to marry him, but he knew it was too soon and I needed time to think about it. The next morning I heard the news that Ranger Landrey had died in a shoot-out. It's all I've been able to think about, to the point that it has torn me apart."

"In other words, you didn't give Luckey an answer."

"No."

Her father eyed her kindly. "Ally? I'm going to tell you something I haven't even told your mother, because it sounds cold and final. You two are my angels and I would never want to hurt you, but this has to be said because it's a bald fact."

She and her mom shared a glance.

"We're *all* going to die, honey."

Ally was listening. "I know."

"You don't think I haven't worried that your mother might go before me? The fear of losing a loved one plagues every human being born on this earth. A few people allow that fear to prevent them from reaching out for happiness."

"Luckey's ex-wife divorced him rather than end up a widow."

"And look what she missed." Beatrice smiled.

Her husband nodded. "Frankly, I was afraid your mother wouldn't accept my proposal because she knew I had another interest besides ranching, one that had the potential to be dangerous. It took a strong woman to take me on."

Beatrice kissed his jaw. "It took a woman in love. After thinking about it, I decided to go wherever you went for as long as I could have you, even if it turned out to be for a short time. I didn't want to miss the experience."

They were so right. Ally was in awe of her parents' wisdom.

"Honey, we're not going to worry if you turn Luckey down. Another man will come along who will have a safer occupation and you'll—"

"No, Dad," she blurted. "You've made your point. *No one's safe.*"

A look of satisfaction broke out on his face. "It's a hard lesson to digest, but a necessary one to help you make the right choice for you."

"Truthfully, after Luckey and I ran into each other

at my office, my heart already knew what it wanted. I've got to go and tell him."

"You don't want our approval?" Larry teased.

"I saw it tonight when Mom threw her arms around him. I also heard it the night Luckey ate dinner with us and you said, 'Your Ranger is the reason why they're still legendary.'"

Ally dashed out of the room and up the stairs to get her purse. There was no time to primp. She worried he'd gone to headquarters, but since it was Sunday, he might have gone home. She hurried out to her car and headed to his house, taking the chance that he might be there.

On the way she debated phoning him. But he might not pick up when he saw the caller ID. Ally decided it would be better if she didn't. Maybe the element of surprise would work in her favor. If he *did* answer the phone, he'd probably tell her this wasn't a good time. She'd never forget the foreboding look on his face after their discussion at his father's party.

There was only one thing she could do to take that look away and that meant showing him in person how in love she was with him, how she couldn't live without him.

His car wasn't visible when she pulled into his driveway. Had he parked in the garage? She drove around to the barn. His truck and trailer were there. She got out and walked inside the lofty structure. Persey nickered, drawing her over to his stall.

"Hey there, Persey. Did you have fun yesterday?" She rubbed his forelock and he nickered again. "Sil-

ver loved the party and didn't want to go home. Neither did I." Ally pressed her head against him. "I wish
you could tell me if Luckey's home."

"He's home," said a deep, familiar male voice.

She spun around, glimpsing his tall silhouette in
the semidarkness. She whispered his name.

"Why didn't you ring the bell?"

Her breath caught. "I didn't know if your car was
in the garage, so I—I thought I'd look here first,"
she stammered.

He didn't make a move toward her. "Have you
come on official business?"

"Official?" Her voice practically squeaked.

"Something to do with the case? Something your
folks thought I needed to know?"

"Yes," Ally answered in a burst of inspiration. "In
a way this *is* official."

"You should have saved yourself the trouble and
phoned me instead."

She stuffed her hands in her back pockets. "What
I have to say should be said face-to-face."

"Go ahead," he replied, after shifting his weight.
"I'm listening."

He wasn't making this easy. "I came to tell you
I'm in love with you, Luckey Davis with an *e*, and I
don't want to live without you."

Luckey stood there like a block of petrified wood.
"In other words you're telling me you'll marry a man
who already has a target on his back."

"A very wise man told me we're *all* living targets,
but you have to get on with life and embrace it to the

fullest for the time you're given. So, yes!" she cried in a tremulous voice. "I want to be your wife no matter when your time is up."

His eyes narrowed on her features. "That's quite a change of heart within the last twenty-four hours. Unfortunately, I jumped the gun by bringing up marriage. Now *I'm* the one having second thoughts." His words stabbed her like a dagger.

"Because I didn't say yes immediately?"

"No." He sounded as if he meant it. "Though your silence hurt in ways you'll never know, I got a taste of what you were feeling when you entered the orphanage to bring Shan out. Anything could have happened to you during that sting, something I hadn't anticipated that could have ended your life prematurely."

"But nothing went wrong, Luckey, and—"

"And nothing!" he interrupted. "Until I saw you drive up to your parents' home with Shan, I couldn't breathe. During that time while I waited for you, I imagined all the horrific things that could have happened to you. I suffered the way I'm sure my ex-wife suffered when I walked out the door every day. I never understood it until I realized you might not make it home.

"Since that moment I've had time to think. I should never have let you talk me into allowing you to go inside the orphanage to talk to Shan. I've regretted it ever since. The only reason my boss was willing to let me use you to help her escape was because you translated the writing on the cheongsam and were deeply involved in the case. But from now on you're out of the whole thing."

Ally started to tremble. "So what are you saying? That you don't want to see me ever again?"

"Want has nothing to do with it." His wintry voice had a debilitating effect on her. "I can't do my work when I'm worried about you."

"I understand." But she wasn't about to let him get away with it. "As long as I'm here, can I be of any help on the case before I drive home?"

"It's best you leave, Ally. I'll walk you to your car."

Crushed by the way he was treating her, she turned to his horse. "I'll see you later, Persey." She patted his rump before walking ahead of Luckey. But when she reached the car, she didn't get in. On impulse she turned to him.

"I'm free tonight. You said you had to get back to work. Give me a job and I'll do it. No one wants Robert Martin put away forever more than I do. Two people doing research together will make things go faster."

His well-defined chest rose and fell. "I can't let you do that."

"Well, I'm going to do it anyway, whether you like it or not!" she retorted. "In the beginning you came to me for help. I went to Houston with you. Now that you've gotten me involved, I'm committed all the way. Let's agree to keep emotions out of it. Give me any assignment. Mom and I tried to do our little part over the years, but at this stage I can really help to make a difference.

"Though you're already a whiz kid at Chinese, you know you could use an expert, if only to make a phone call here or there or to provide backup for translation. Use me, Luckey, because I'm not leaving here. In fact, I'm going to text my teaching assistant and ask him to cover for me tomorrow, too. That way I can work through the night with you if necessary."

"No, Ally!" Luckey snapped, but she ignored him.

After sending the message, she lifted her head. "Why?" She continued the argument, sensing that he was starting to cave. "Last week you said, and I quote, 'I need to solve this case ASAP so I can have a normal life with you.' Remember?"

His lips thinned in an uncompromising line.

"I have a photographic memory, too, Ranger Davis." Ally walked to the front of his house and stood at the door to wait for him. "While we're here together working like crazy, neither of us is in danger, so there's no problem."

"The hell there isn't."

She bit the inside of her bottom lip so she wouldn't smile. "We'll make a new rule. Three feet away from each other at all times, and if you have to leave on an emergency, I'll stay put and take care of Persey until you get back."

His sharp intake of breath didn't escape her. "This isn't funny, Ally."

"It kind of is," she answered, then challenged him. "Shall we see how long we last before we realize how ridiculous it is to fight something we know we're going to lose, *Kemo Sabe*?"

She'd purposely called him Tonto's nickname for the Lone Ranger in order to trigger a reaction, and she got one. His body started to shake with laughter before it pealed out of him.

"That's more like it." Ally smiled at him. She loved this man with a passion. "Come on and show me what you were working on when I interrupted you by showing up in your driveway. Chop chop!" She slapped her hands together several times in succession.

"Don't tell me that's a Chinese expression," he drawled.

"No. It's one of mine, because I'm hoping to get this show on the road. Are you always going to be this difficult?"

A glimmer of amusement lingered in his eyes. He opened the door. "It's evident there are many sides to you not immediately apparent. Won't you come in, Dr. Duncan."

Ally was so happy to have won this skirmish she practically floated into his house without her feet touching the ground.

LUCKEY USHERED HER into his den. "I'll make a place for you at the end of the desk so you can see the screen, too." He pulled up another chair for her. "I'll bring us some coffee." He had no intention of letting her stay long.

A few minutes later he joined her with mugs of hot brew and snacks. Luckey hadn't been able to say no to her. When she'd driven over to his place, determined to tell him she would marry him, he'd been afraid to believe it. He wanted her for his wife more than anything he'd wanted in his whole life.

But everything he'd told her about his fear for her safety was true. Until she'd arrived at her parents' home with Shan, he'd been frightened out of his mind. Her life was so precious to him, it had caused him to question if he could handle marrying this woman. If he lost her…

"Where do you want to start?"

"I'll check any new emails, then we'll dig in." One of the messages in his in-box had come from a Chinese Olympic official, who had sent a telephone number. "I'm making progress, Ally," Luckey stated. "This person should be able to give me information about gymnastics training in China."

Her eyes met his. "Do you think he'll be willing to tell you everything you want to know? Does he realize you're a Texas Ranger?"

"Not yet. I asked someone official to supply me with a name of someone dealing with the Junior Olympic team, but I didn't give a reason for my inquiry."

"Then why don't you let me talk to him. I'll think up a story that won't make him suspicious."

"What kind of excuse will you use?"

"I'll pretend to be a Chinese mother returning to Changsha. I'm trying to find the best trainer for my fourteen-year-old gymnast daughter, who wants to make the team. Could he put me in touch with the right people?"

Ally was one of those people who thought out of

the box. She was an original with a wonderful mind. If anyone could pull it off, she could. The man on the other end wouldn't have a clue she was an American.

Luckey nodded. "I'm replying to his message as we speak. I've told him a Chinese woman will be contacting him by phone. You take it from there and we'll see how much information you can get out of him."

"Thank you for letting me do this." Her eyes shone with a heavenly blue luster. A man could lose his soul in them.

"Call him when you're ready." Luckey gave her a pen and pad to make notes if she needed to.

Five minutes later he was listening to a lengthy conversation she'd put on speaker so he could hear both ends. He doubted many foreigners ever mastered Chinese the way she had. Luckey marveled at her expertise. Their talk went on for quite a while. She asked dozens of questions the man on the other end willingly answered. Ally made a number of notes. He did recognize the words *xiexie ni* before she hung up. They meant thank you.

Her gaze collided with his. "He was a gold mine, Luckey. We now have the names, numbers and addresses of the best trainers in China."

The three-feet-apart boundary Ally had set for them went out the window the moment he reached over to cover her hand and squeeze it. "You are a master of deception. If I'd been on the phone with him, our conversation probably wouldn't have lasted more than a couple of minutes and I'd have had little to show for it."

Her eyes gleamed. "I'm so glad I learned Chinese the way I did, if only to find the man who brought about Yu Tan's death. I'm going to start making more phone calls and fish around for any information."

Luckey released her hand with reluctance. "You're right, Ally. Two people working together makes the job go so much faster."

For the next few minutes he listened to her have several phone conversations, and watched her jot down more notes. While she was still on the phone, he went to the kitchen and made some grilled cheese sandwiches to keep them going. He brought them to the den along with fresh coffee, and waited for her to hang up.

"What do you think? Did you learn anything helpful?"

"Not yet, but I've got one more person on the list to phone." She reached for a sandwich. "Thanks for this. I didn't realize how hungry I was." She placed her last call. His interest piqued when a quick back-and-forth question-and-answer session ensued. He could tell she was on to something.

Again he heard *xiexie ni* before she clicked off. Ally shot him a glance. "I asked this trainer how the girl gymnasts get picked. He told me talent scouts circulate throughout China trying to find the most promising ones at the various schools. When I inquired further, he gave me names of three scouts. Here they are. I've written their Chinese equivalents so you can understand them."

Ally passed him her notepad. When he looked

down, one stood out in blazing letters: *Sima Wang.*
That was Robert Martin's stepfather.

"Ally? Do me a favor and call the man back.
Ask him to tell you anything he knows about Sima
Wang—where he lives, how often he's in China. Get
a description if you can."

She stared at Luckey. "All right, but I'll have to be
cagey." After placing the call, she again conversed
back and forth. Finally, Ally thanked the man and
rang off. "He said Sima Wang is a dark blond American, and rich. He lives somewhere in China and
is probably in his forties. Every so often he comes
around to Hunan Province. About five weeks ago he
was in Changsha, giving a demonstration in kung fu."

*ROBERT MARTIN HAD taken on his stepfather's name
while he perpetrated his evil in China. Robert's birth
parents were dead. Were his adoptive parents dead,
as well? Had he killed them, too?*

Luckey jumped out of the chair. "You found him,
Ally!" He pulled her into his arms and swung her
around. "We've got him. You did it!"

"But how do you know?"

He carried her over to the couch and lay down
next to her, trapping her legs with his own. For a little while he lost track of time, kissing her. Finally,
he lifted his head to look down at her. "First things
first. Where did you come from? Out of all the men
in the world, how was I lucky enough to meet you?"

She kissed his mouth with a hunger that thrilled
him down to the last cell in his body. "The real ques-

tion is how is it possible that out of all the Chinese experts you could have talked to, you came to me first? I love you so much."

"You're my heart, Ally. My love for you knows no bounds."

A bewitching smile appeared on her face. "I notice you forgot our rule to stay three feet away."

"No more rules. Sweetheart…" He kissed her again and again, unable to stop. "We have to get married as soon as I arrest Wang. My boss will give me time off for a long honeymoon. We're going to need it. The way I'm feeling right now, we may never come back."

"Oh, yes, we will. As your mother reminded me, you're a restless man, but I've already accepted that fact. Now tell me how you know Sima Wang is the man you've been looking for."

Luckey buried his face in Ally's neck. "I can't think while you're in my arms."

"I could stay like this forever, too, but I want to get married. The sooner we can make an arrest, the sooner we can do that."

Ally was a living, breathing miracle. He devoured her one more time, then eased himself off her and got to his feet. He reached for her hands to pull her up. "Come on, slave driver. You've motivated me to stay on track until this is finished, so I'm depending on you to keep me focused."

She threw her arms around his neck. "I'd do anything for you."

"My feelings exactly."

They kissed with growing passion before he found

the strength to let her go. Once they sat down at the desk again, she looked at her notepad and tapped Wang's name. "Why do you know he's the one?"

"That day I went to Freeport, I learned that Sima Wang was the name of Martin's Chinese adoptive father."

"You're kidding!"

Luckey went on to explain everything he'd learned about the man. "It appears Martin has taken over in Sima's stead. No doubt the adoptive father is dead."

"You think he killed him?"

"Maybe. His adoptive mother could be dead, too."

Luckey could hear Ally's mind working. "Are his birth parents still alive?" she asked.

"No. I found a record of their deaths in Freeport."

"What was her name? Maybe he operates there when he's in the States."

Luckey shook his head. "I've already done a thorough search. Nothing showed up. To answer your question, her name was Sybil Martin Mott. I looked for any Martins or Motts living in Freeport or the surrounding areas, but came up with nothing."

Ally wrote the woman's name on her pad. Her delicately arched brows formed a frown. "Let's do a statewide search of all Martins and Motts."

"I love your energy, sweetheart, but we won't be able to get into that database before morning."

"Then let's keep going through the last few names on the carriers' list of deliveries. Martin's hands were on Yu Tan's body before she was brought into the morgue. I keep thinking about Soo-Lin's letter. She talked about Yu Tan's friend who said she'd gotten involved with a man at a disco club. Maybe Martin threatened her friend, who saw the abduction. He could have forced her to make up that story, threatening to kill her and her family."

"I have no doubt of it."

"He has to be hiding out here someplace close when he's in Texas." Luckey felt Ally shudder. "He's evil."

"After stealing eight million dollars, he has the money to go where he wants and live the way he likes. His job looking over new gymnast prospects gives him the perfect opportunity to handpick the girls he wants for his operation. We know he was in Jakarta because of the testimony from the Indonesian girl rescued from the spa. With China and Indonesia as his oysters, he's set up a widespread ring using various aliases, an operation that could go on for years if he isn't stopped."

"You'll catch him and I'm going to help you."

With Ally at his side, Luckey could believe it.

"Can I see all his aliases?"

He handed her the sheet in the file folder. "So," she said, studying them, "we're looking for either Dino Morten, Bobo Marten, Sid Marteen, Momo Demott, Angelo Martin or Sima Wang."

"Or even another alias that hasn't shown up on the rap sheet," Luckey murmured.

"They're such bizarre names."

"He puts on kung fu shows and probably uses them like a stage name."

"Of course." Ally reached for Luckey's hand. "No matter how much money you get paid for doing your job, it couldn't possibly be enough. But I know you're not in it for the money, so I'm sorry I brought it up. I admire you so much, Luckey."

Her voice broke, causing him to lean close and kiss her for a long time before they got back to work.

"Let's start by tracking down the last of these deliveries.

"I'll write the addresses and names on my pad for quick reference."

"Tomorrow we'll call each number to find out what information we can."

She watched the screen with him. "It's amazing how many people buy this cream online."

"We've become an online society," he murmured. "Health remedies gross in the millions of dollars. If we can find Martin going this route, I'm going to be more thankful than ever for the internet."

They worked until three in the morning. Ally's eyelids were drooping when Luckey closed the file they'd been working on and sat back in his chair. "Time for bed. My guest bedroom is yours for the night. You know where it is. Sleep as long as you want. Tomorrow we'll make a big breakfast and get started again. Don't ask me to kiss you good-night."

"I know better than to do that." She got up, kissed the top of his head and disappeared out of the den with her purse in hand. Her touch was pure torture and she left a trail of fragrance he couldn't get enough of.

Before he called it a night, he opened an email that had come from the silk merchant in Jakarta.

Re your request: The silk sample is called karawo from Gorontalo. It has become the people's pride, but not so many have it, since karawo is a cultural heritage. Below is the name of my shop in Jakarta that carries it. I am pleased to be of service.

Luckey immediately responded and thanked him. After telling him he was investigating a police matter, he hoped the man could give him the names and addresses of anyone who'd purchased that specific material in the last two years. His request would probably be denied. If so, he'd ask TJ to notify the authorities in Jakarta and issue a warrant in order to obtain the information. But it was worth a try to ask the man first.

With that accomplished, Luckey went to bed. Knowing Ally was safely under his roof, he fell asleep the minute his head touched the pillow.

Chapter Eleven

Ally woke up at nine, excited to have awakened in Luckey's home. She had texted her teaching assistant before going to sleep and told him she would need the week off. He sent back a message saying he had it covered. She slipped across the hall to the guest bathroom to freshen up. When she'd dressed, she headed to the den and realized Luckey must still be in bed. Taking advantage of the time, she hurried to the kitchen and fixed breakfast for the two of them, bacon, eggs and pancakes.

Once she had the coffee brewing, Luckey appeared in the doorway showered and shaved, wearing a golf shirt and jeans. Ally melted to see him walk in the kitchen, and gravitated to him. He kissed her long and hard.

"This is what it's going to be like after we're married," he whispered into her hair. "I don't think I can wait."

"That's why we're going to keep working all day."

He cupped her cheeks. "Have I told you how beautiful you look in the morning?"

"I hope that's always the case," she said. "Where you're concerned, you take my breath away no matter what the hour. Sit down and I'll serve you."

She'd been counting on him having a big appetite and he didn't disappoint her. They ate until he'd finished off the last pancake. After the dishes were done they went to the barn to feed Persey and lead him out to the corral, where he could enjoy the day.

"We'll go riding later." Luckey patted his horse, and then reached for Ally's hand. They headed back inside to the den and he told her about the silk merchant from Jakarta. "I'm hoping he'll give me the information without going through the authorities."

"I wish I spoke Indonesian. Do you know if he speaks Mandarin, too?"

"I didn't think to ask."

"Why don't you call him back? If the answer is yes, I'll talk to him and tell him how crucial it is we learn everything we can. He might be willing to help us."

"If anyone can get him to talk, you can." Luckey reached for his phone and put through the call. "It's gone to his voice mail. I'll leave a message for him to call me back. We'll see what happens. For now, let's get started making phone calls to all those numbers you jotted down last night."

Ally loved working with Luckey. Together they pored over this last list of numbers, discussing each one to see if it was worth investigating. So far Luckey didn't feel any of them set off alarm bells.

At two o'clock he received a phone call from headquarters. He darted her a glance. "One of the guys needs backup. I have to go."

The news disappointed her, but this was Luckey's life. She didn't dare think about what he might be walking into.

"I'll go home and see you later."

He gave her a hard kiss that made her knees buckle. "When I'm through, I'll come by for you and we'll go out to dinner. I owe you after all the work you've done."

"All I want is to be with you." *I love you, love you, love you, Luckey.* That mantra was still on her lips as she put the notebook in her purse and they left the house together. She walked around the side of his home to her car. When she called out to Persey, he neighed. It put a smile on her face during the drive home.

After discovering her folks weren't there, Ally made a sandwich and hurried upstairs to shower and wash her hair. They'd probably left to go visit family before her dad had to fly back to DC on Sunday. She left them a text telling them where she'd been and that she was home, but she would be going out to dinner later with Luckey.

At last she was ready and could start calling the numbers listed. But before she started, she needed to think of a plausible excuse for phoning a stranger, whether it be a business or residence. After coming up with several ideas, she decided on a plan she felt would work and tried it out with the first number.

"Hello. I'm a marketing representative hired by

Gema Pharmaceutical, calling to see if you received your DMSO product and if you're pleased with it." She told them the date she knew it had been delivered, and then asked several questions about who was using it. Did they intend to buy more? How did they rate the product in terms of pain relief? How did they hear about it? Would they buy it again? Were other members of the family using it?

A half-dozen calls revealed the majority of recipients were middle-aged and had seen the company advertised on the internet. She found it amazing how much information they were willing to share about themselves. Though she would go over every set of responses with Luckey after he came for her, she didn't hear anything she thought was important.

Three calls later an elderly woman answered. Ally started out the same way as before, but the woman laughed. "Oh, no, dear, it's not for me. You're asking the wrong person. I have a grandson who has it sent here. It's for him."

Ally's pulse picked up speed. "Is he in a lot of pain?"

"Oh my, yes. He puts on exhibitions around the country, but spends part of every month with me. When he comes home, he uses the cream to soothe his joints."

"That's interesting. What does he do?"

"Oh, I don't remember exactly, and I have macular degeneration so I can't read anymore. When he was little he said he wanted to grow up to be like that Chan fellow in the movies." She laughed again.

Jackie Chan? The Chinese karate expert?

Ally had trouble keeping the tremor out of her voice. "I see. Well, thank you very much for your time. You've been so helpful with this survey. The company appreciates every endorsement. Goodbye."

Ally hung up in shock. *This was it!* She knew it in her bones.

Luckey hadn't phoned yet, and it was still light out. She double-checked the address for Vera Jarvis and decided to take a drive past her house. The woman lived in the downtown area of Austin. Ally couldn't wait to tell Luckey, but she didn't dare disturb him. Instead she sent him a text.

I'm positive I've found Robert Martin through his supposed grandmother, Vera Jarvis! I've left to drive by the address and check it out. Call me the second you can!

A few minutes later she headed downtown and before long found the house where Vera Jarvis lived. It looked as though it had been built in the 1960s, but for an older home it was nicely kept up. Ally took several pictures with her phone and then parked across the street, in front of another house farther down, to wait until Luckey contacted her. Fifteen minutes went by, and the next thing she knew it had been an hour. Still no word from him. As she'd learned the night Ranger Landrey had been shot, it could be tomorrow before she heard from Luckey.

For the first time in her life she had an idea of what

a police crew went through when they put a house under surveillance. The waiting for something, anything, to happen grew old in a hurry. Her chances of spotting Martin when he happened to be in Austin were probably one in a million, but it didn't matter. She was here now and planned to sit this out for as long as she could.

Cars went by. A few people came home from work and entered driveways. She wished she'd brought a snack with her. Around six her mom texted her to say they'd gone to her uncle Nick's and would be home by nine. Another text came in from Ally's assistant at the university. He'd emailed her some department information. Ally texted him back to thank him.

As she lifted her head, she saw a new black Ford Explorer turn into the older woman's driveway and enter the garage. No. Way. Ally couldn't believe she hadn't seen the driver or glimpsed the license plate in time. Was it Martin? Or a caregiver, maybe? Did anyone else live with Vera Jarvis? The woman might require help.

While Ally waited to see if anything would happen, she texted Luckey again with details about the Explorer. By eight o'clock she realized it was pointless to stay put any longer and started her car. But no sooner did she signal to pull out into traffic than she saw the Explorer back out of the driveway and whip right past her.

At this point her heart started beating like a jackhammer. She followed the SUV from a distance. Before long the driver headed out on US Highway 183 toward the airport. Then, to her surprise, he unexpectedly turned into a gated, grubby looking warehouse in the 7900 block. A high chain-link fence surrounded the entire property. There were half a dozen cars parked haphazardly beneath old oak trees.

Ally slowed down to watch the car pull up to one end of the medium-sized building. It was dark now, with only minimal lighting, but she could tell it was a tallish man who got out and went inside. Her adrenaline picked up as she pulled into a closed service station across the street. She turned off her lights and waited to see if anything else was going to happen. While she sat there she sent another text to Luckey, letting him know this address.

Forty-five minutes passed before she saw a different SUV, not the Ford, come around from the back of the warehouse. When the gates opened, the driver turned down the highway toward the city. Why hadn't Luckey texted her back yet?

She started her car and took off after it. Her heart was in her throat by the time it turned into an alley off Lamar Boulevard. Ally didn't dare follow. She made a U-turn to backtrack and saw the sign for a Chinese massage parlor on her right.

Ally knew in her gut another poor victim had just been delivered from that warehouse. She texted the location of the massage parlor to Luckey. This was how Martin did it. He brought in girls from the airport and took them to the warehouse. From there they were driven to whatever vile place he picked. Yu Tan had been held at that warehouse. Before she could be taken to a place like this, she'd tried to escape and had been shot.

Those poor girls…

Wild with fury for what he'd done to them, Ally took off for the warehouse once more, to keep an eye on Martin. But when she reached the service station and pulled in, she saw that the black Ford Explorer had gone. Were there any girls being held in there tonight? Filled with anguish, she was too slow to realize two Caucasian men had approached her from the shadows. They were armed with assault rifles. "Get out of the car!" they ordered.

Her hands froze on the wheel. Time to use her wits. "I'm lost, looking for someone. Please let me go."

Suddenly one of the men shattered the side window with the butt of his rifle and opened her door. Glass grazed her cheek. The other man dragged her out of the car and tied a foul-smelling cloth around her mouth. He pulled her across the highway to the gate, which he unlocked with a remote device. The man who'd broken the window held her purse and phone. She'd stumbled into a nightmare.

They took her into a small office and tied her to the chair behind the desk. The man holding her purse ripped through her bag and tore her wallet apart. "Well, look who we have here. Allison Forrester Duncan, age 28, five foot seven, eyes blue, address Crystal Mountain Road." He whistled. "Ritzy. What's a gorgeous babe like you doing slumming around here this time of night in that fancy car?"

Ally made sounds while the other man checked out

her cell phone. "I'll tell you what she's been doing. She's been spying on the boss and sending messages. He's not going to like it when he hears about this. I'll call him while you take her out back. Don't rough her up too much until he tells us what he wants done with her."

"We don't have any more empty rooms."

"Then throw her in with one of the girls."

The man untied her hands and dragged her through another door. After leading her down a long hallway with doors on both sides, he unlocked one and threw her inside, knocking her to the cement floor. She heard a shuffling sound in the room before the door clanged shut.

A small vent to the outside near the ceiling prevented the space from being completely black. Over in the corner huddled a figure. Ally got up on her knees and made her way to her. In a minute the girl undid the cloth and it fell away.

"Xie xie," Ally said to her in Mandarin. "My name is Ally. I'm here to help you. The man I'm going to marry is a policeman. Soon he will come and get us out of here. While we're alone, tell me everything you can about what has happened to you."

The girl broke into a spate of Chinese, speaking so fast Ally had trouble following her. They must have been there, talking, for an hour before they heard the door open. Someone shone a flashlight in their faces. Ally was jerked to her feet and dragged down the hall to the same office as before.

This time a light had been turned on. She found

herself looking into the cold hazel eyes of a tall, dark blond, athletic-looking man. "So *you're* Robert Martin, the dragon with the split yellow tongue. To refresh your memory, you're wanted for murder, armed robbery and female trafficking. You're without a doubt the most depraved man on the planet," she spat out.

He gave her a stinging slap across the face that cut her lip and would leave bruises, but her outrage was stronger than her fear.

"You know how I can tell?" she asked, baiting him. "You reek of garlic from the cream you use. I can smell the stench from here. That's what gave you away."

His eyes narrowed to slits. "You're the woman who duped my grandmother on the phone."

"What happened to your adoptive father and aunt? Did you kill them, too? Does your grandmother know about that? Your days of rounding up female gymnasts like cattle has come to an end. You can kill me, but it won't stop the Texas Rangers from putting you away for the rest of your unnatural life."

He screwed up his face. "The Texas Rangers don't know squat about me."

"Want to make a bet? Who do you think received all those text messages I sent?"

A nervous tic played havoc with the corner of his mouth. "You're lying," he growled. "Who are you?"

"I'm the daughter of Lawrence Duncan, former ambassador to China for fifteen years, until last summer when he was recalled to the States. Your entire operation throughout Asia is going to be closed down, sending the hundreds of evil kidnappers who work for you to prison.

"Surely by now you must know you're the top man on the FBI's most-wanted list, Bobo. Or shall I call you Momo? Perhaps your greatest act will be to face the death penalty for your crimes against humanity. Thousands of families of female victims will cheer."

His skin grew mottled with rage. He lunged for her and knocked her against the wall. Just before she blacked out, Rangers swarmed the room. She cried out Luckey's name before everything went dark.

THE PARAMEDIC IN the ambulance finished putting in the IV. "She's coming to, sir."

Luckey hunkered next to her, holding her free hand. He kissed it. "Ally, sweetheart? I'm right here."

Her head moved back and forth before her eyes opened. "Luckey..." Her voice broke with emotion. Tears streamed out of the corners of her eyes.

"It's all over. You're going to be fine, thank God. Do you know you captured Robert Martin single-handedly? Everyone from the warehouse is in custody." Luckey had so much to tell her, he didn't know where to start, but right now she needed rest and quiet.

"You got all my messages?"

"Every one of them. But I didn't hear from you again after I reached the massage parlor, and I couldn't figure out where you'd gone. By then the Rangers had taken over and had followed your leads. All I could do was obey my instinct and meet the guys at the warehouse.

"When I saw your car and heard you baiting Martin, I couldn't get to you fast enough. You're the smartest, bravest woman I ever met, but if you ever do this to me again, I swear I'll die of a heart attack."

"Please don't do that. Now we can get married, right?"

He sucked in his breath. "Right, but I'd like to live long enough to enjoy the honeymoon."

"Where shall we go?"

"I don't know yet. I can't think."

"Wherever we go, let's take the horses."

"You're a girl after my own heart. Now try to rest. We'll be at the hospital in a minute. I've already notified your parents. They'll meet us there."

"I don't want to go to the hospital. Just take me back to your house."

The paramedic grinned. "You're one lucky dude," he said.

"You can say that again," Luckey whispered back, before squeezing Ally's hand. After kissing her cheek, he told her, "You need to be checked out by a doctor first. You took a big risk confronting Martin on your own."

"When I thought of what he did to Yu Tan, something inside me snapped."

"It certainly did." Luckey smiled through his tears, so proud of what she'd done he was ready to burst. "I'm sure he's never been taken on by a woman like you in his whole evil life."

"I was thrown in a back room with one of the young girls. She gave me a lot of information."

"I'll get it from you later. You probably have a concussion and need to stop talking. Tonight Cy told me he thinks you're in the wrong profession and need to come work with us. But I told him I prefer calling you Dr. Duncan. You're the only woman I want."

"All that matters to me is to be your wife."

The ambulance pulled into the hospital entrance and she was rushed inside the emergency room. Luckey hung back while Beatrice and Larry ran over to her, before she was wheeled into a cubicle so the doctor could examine her. Her father lifted his head and the two men exchanged glances.

"Your daughter is one in a million. She brought Robert Martin down and deserves all the praise in the world."

"Our daughter has always seized the moment. That's her nature, to go where angels fear to tread. But it takes two to pull off this kind of a coup. She's more than met her match in you, Ranger Davis. I don't know how to thank you enough for saving her life." Larry walked over and hugged Luckey. The moment turned out to be an emotional one for both of them.

Beatrice came out from behind the curtain and threw her arms around Luckey. "You wonderful man." Her quiet sobs warmed his heart.

"If you'd seen and heard her stand up to Martin, you'd know where the definition of *wonderful* comes from." He eyed both Ally's parents. "I know it's only been two weeks, but do I have your permission to marry her when she's all better?"

"Do you even have to ask?" Larry murmured.

Luckey breathed a sigh of relief. "Just making sure."

His three best buddies walked into the emergency room with smiles, and headed for them. There were more hugs all around. When her parents left to go join Ally, Kit pulled Luckey aside with the guys.

"I don't think you know what you've done. We went into the grandmother's house with a search warrant. That killer has a whole porn site set up for his base of operations, to the tune of twenty-five thousand clients."

Luckey whistled.

"So far we've discovered he owns a dozen spas and massage parlors from here to Houston," Vic interjected. "The one off Lamar Boulevard is being closed down as we speak. Twenty girls have been given their freedom."

"That's where he gets the money to keep funding his operations," Cy theorized. "His poor grandmother had no idea. This is the biggest ring ever to be brought down. TJ is higher than a kite over what you've done."

"Ally's the one who led us to him, but there are two people who deserve the greatest credit." The guys stared at him. "Dr. Wolff and Stan. I swear that our forensics experts help us get our man every time. Dr. Wolff found the DMSO cream on the girl's sleeves. Stan found where it was manufactured. Those two deserve a medal."

Vic eyed Luckey with a gleam in his black eyes. "Before this whole business is finished and put to bed, I suspect a whole lot of medals are going to be given out."

Luckey got a lump in his throat. "Thanks, guys."

Kit smiled. "We'll get out of your way. Let us know when you decide to tie the knot. We want to be there. Unless you pull a Cy and get a judge to marry you on the sly."

Luckey's brows lifted. "I'm all for it, but that's up to Ally."

"TJ said for you to take off all the time you need."

"Thanks, Kit. I'll call him after the doctor lets me talk to Ally."

He watched them walk out of the emergency room. No man ever had better friends.

In a few minutes Ally's parents hurried toward him. "The doctor is sending her to room 312," Beatrice explained. "You can see her up there. He'll keep her in the hospital through tomorrow night for observation. She has a light concussion, but he's certain she'll recover without complications. Larry and I are going home, but we'll be back tomorrow."

The good news helped him to relax. Luckey gave Ally's mom another hug before they left the emergency room. While Ally's parents headed for the parking lot, he found the bank of elevators and pressed the button for the third floor. When he reached the nursing station, he asked if housekeeping could bring a cot to room 312. He had no intention of leaving Ally for any reason.

She still hadn't arrived when he entered the room. Deciding to take advantage of the time, he texted

TJ to let him know he was at the hospital with Ally and all was well. It was 5:30 a.m. His boss had to be asleep, but he'd see the message when he woke up.

Next, Luckey texted his parents and Randy to let them know the case he'd been working on had been solved and he'd get back to them later in the day with all the news. There was no point telling them about Ally. They'd hear everything later.

Finally, he fired off a text to Art, the teenager next door, asking him to take care of Persey until further notice. Luckey had barely finished it when Ally was wheeled into the room.

"Luckey…" Her smile lit up his universe.

It didn't matter that she had a cut lip. She was so breathtaking he would always marvel.

"Sweetheart."

"I have to stay here until tomorrow. Please don't leave me."

"As if I would." No sooner had he spoken than his cot was delivered. While he set it aside, a nurse came in to make Ally comfortable and take her vital signs and check the IV put in during the ambulance ride. After typing the information into the computer, she left them alone.

Luckey drew the chair over to Ally's side and clasped her free hand, kissing the palm. "I just spoke to your parents. They've gone home to get some sleep, but they'll be back later."

"I know. I'm glad we're alone. If you don't mind, I want to talk to you about something very serious."

His heart lurched. "What is it? Did that monster do something else to you I don't know about?"

"No…" She shook her head. "This has to do with you and me. Please hear me out."

Ally… "Tell me."

"Tonight I realized how fast a life can be snuffed out. In an instant anything can go wrong. That girl at the warehouse. One minute she was walking home from school. The next minute she was kidnapped and her world turned upside down." Ally squeezed his hand hard. "Every moment is so precious I don't want to waste a second. If you really want to marry me, would you be willing for us to get married here in the hospital?"

His mind reeled back to Kit's earlier comment about Cy getting married to Kellie on the sly because they couldn't wait.

"What if you and I only have a few days together before something happens to one of us?" She lifted her head off the pillow and turned to him with urgency. "What if we only have a week or a month? I don't want to plan a big wedding that takes forever. The important thing is to be your wife right now. When the doctor releases me, I want to go home with you to your house, belonging to you in every way. We can use the nurses for witnesses. That way no one in our families, on either side, gets hurt because we didn't include them."

Ally was deadly serious. He felt it and saw it. They were soul mates. The joy her words brought left him close to speechless.

"Tell you what. If you'll go to sleep now, I'll see what I can do to arrange it."

"Promise?"

"What do you think?" He leaned over to kiss one side of her mouth.

Before long he could tell she'd fallen asleep. He pulled out his cell and called information for his friend Judge Montoya. Good old Montoya always helped out in a crisis. This was Luckey's biggest one to date.

His call rang through to the judge's office voice mail. Luckey identified himself and asked him to phone back ASAP about performing a quick marriage for him and Ally at the hospital. He knew it would be on a Tuesday, but would he do it? That would get his attention in a big hurry.

After clicking off, Luckey opened the cot and pulled off his boots. He whipped the pillow into shape, then stretched out with a deep sigh, facing Ally.

The judge called back late the next day, while Luckey and Ally were eating dinner with Ally's parents. After he explained his dilemma, the Judge said he could arrange for a special license for them. But the ceremony would have to take place tomorrow morning at eight before he went out of town. Luckey thanked him and clicked off before letting out a whoop of excitement.

"Will he do it?" she cried.

"Eight o'clock in the morning."

"You're serious."

"It's too late to take back what you asked for."

"I can't believe it!"

"Ally—while your parents are still here, I'm going to leave to do some errands and run home to shower. I'll be back tonight."

"Okay. But hurry!"

He brushed her lips gently with his own before he left the hospital. His world was about to change forever.

Chapter Twelve

By six in the morning Ally was wide-awake. This was her wedding day! She felt fantastic. The bump on the back of her head was disappearing. Her IV had been removed. She looked over at Luckey, who lay sleeping on the cot.

Her clean-shaven Ranger had come back to the hospital late last night. He was wearing a cream-colored shirt and black pants she hadn't seen before. They'd said only a few words and kissed before they'd both fallen asleep.

One of the nurses came in with a new flower arrangement and handed Ally the card. It was written in Luckey's hand. *"For my beautiful bride on our wedding day."* She buried her face in the flowers and shed tears of joy before the nurse put them on one of the carts.

Ally's parents arrived. Her mother had brought a fresh change of clothes for her to wear home from the hospital. A clean pair of jeans and a print blouse would be her wedding attire. With the other woman's help, she went to the restroom and showered. When she came out, they ate breakfast. They arranged that Luckey would take her home from the hospital.

Ally told the nurse that a circuit court judge would be arriving soon, because she and Luckey were getting married within the hour. Would she please find another nurse and both stand as witnesses for the ceremony?

At twenty to eight Luckey woke up. He sat up with a jerk, as if disoriented. Ally's parents smiled.

"Good morning, my love. The judge will be here any minute."

"I can't believe I slept this long."

"You're exhausted, that's why."

Luckey stood up and folded the cot, rolling it against the wall.

"Come sit by me and eat. We've all eaten."

He kissed her cheek before pulling up a chair to tuck in. "You look radiant. How are you feeling?"

"Wonderful. I'm ready to go home with you. Last night the doctor said he'd release me during his morning rounds."

"I'm still pinching myself that this dream of mine is about to happen."

"And it's too late to change your mind," a distinctive male voice declared from the doorway. The judge was followed by two nurses.

Luckey smiled. "That couldn't happen. Allison Duncan, meet Judge Carlos Montoya, the man who has been kind enough to drop everything in order to marry us, on a Wednesday no less."

"We're so thankful, Judge." Her voice shook.

His eyes lit up when he looked at Ally. "I can see why your husband-to-be is in such a terrible hurry."

"Actually, I'm the one who begged him to marry me before I left the hospital. You're doing us such a great favor. One day soon we'll find a way to repay you."

"It's my pleasure to see that Luckey has finally found himself the right woman. He's the best of the best, but you already know that, right?" The older man winked at Ally.

"That's exactly who he is."

"All right. Let's get started. Do you need to stay in bed? Or can you stand up long enough for the short ceremony I'm about to perform?"

"I can stand." She slid off the mattress.

"Luckey? Take her hand."

He grasped it and could probably feel her heart beating throughout his body. Her parents also stood.

"Dearly beloved, what a glorious day is about to begin for you. Two people joined as one to be friends, comforters and lovers throughout this life and the next. Man wasn't meant to go through life alone. Cherish the families who have helped make you who you are. Treasure this gift of marriage that has been given to you. Bless it with children. Honor it with your fidelity. Strive to make the other happy and you will have joy. Now repeat after me…"

They exchanged their vows.

"I now pronounce you man and wife in the eyes of God, these witnesses and the laws of Travis County, Texas. Do you have rings to exchange?"

Ally had forgotten about that, but not her amazing husband-to-be. He pulled two rings out of his pocket and put them on the ring finger of her left hand. She gasped at the large purple solitaire diamond set in gold sitting next to the gold wedding band.

"You can kiss her now."

Luckey gave her a peck on one side of her mouth. "I would have given her a longer one, but she has a cut lip. If I were to kiss her the way I need to…"

The judge chuckled. "I hear you." He pulled a form out of his briefcase and placed it on the table extending over the bed. "If you ladies will put your signatures here…" he said to the nurses. Once the papers were signed, the older man thanked the two women for their participation.

After they left, Ally took her turn signing the wedding certificate. Then Luckey placed his signature on the document, while she shook the judge's hand. "Those words were simple and beautiful. We'll never forget this day. Thank you so much."

"It was the perfect ceremony," Luckey told him.

"So…the deed is done. Congratulations. I hope you'll be very happy."

"We already are," Ally rushed to assure him.

Luckey shook the older man's hand and walked him out to the corridor with Ally's parents.

She looked at the document they'd just signed. It was official. As soon as she was released, she was going home with the man she adored.

Luckey strode back in with fire in those dark brown eyes and drew her into his arms. "The doctor will be right in to check you over one last time, Mrs. Davis."

Mrs. Davis. What beautiful words.

Ally clung to him, burying her face against his neck and shoulder. "I didn't know I could be this happy."

"Just wait till I get you home."

LUCKEY PULLED ALONGSIDE the house. He would have driven into the garage, but he wanted to carry his new bride over the threshold. With his heart pumping like crazy, he opened the passenger door and picked her up.

"Welcome home, sweetheart." In a few steps he reached the front door and used his remote to let them inside. "I'll bring our things in a minute." He shut the door and carried her down the hall to his bedroom.

Ally let out a small cry. "Oh, Luckey—so many flowers! How did you have time to do all this?"

"I asked my cleaning lady, Ruth, to get things ready for us. New sheets on the bed, new towels in the bathroom. All the food we'd want to eat in the fridge. For the next forty-eight hours there's a big Do Not Disturb sign at the Davis residence." He laid her down gently on the bed. "I'll be right back."

"Luckey?" she murmured. "I'm not made of glass, you know."

"But you've just come home from the hospital." He kissed her forehead and hurried out to the car to bring in her overnight bag and the flowers. When he walked back into the bedroom he found his wife texting someone.

She looked up. "I just told Mom and Dad that you've brought me home. In a few days we'll come by the ranch."

"While the doctor gave you a last checkup, I texted my folks."

"Oh, good."

"Great minds think alike." He put her overnight bag on a chair and opened it for her. "While you get ready for bed, I'll bring in some food. Ruth makes wonderful fajitas. All I have to do is warm them up."

If Ally said anything, he didn't hear her as he went out to the kitchen, nervous as hell. This wasn't the way he'd planned for their honeymoon to start out, but the doctor had warned him to treat her carefully. Once he'd prepared a tray, he took their meal into the bedroom and set it on the dresser.

He shouldn't have been surprised that she'd already gotten under the covers. Recovering from a concussion, even if it had been a light one, meant bed still felt good to her. But there was something different about Ally. An energy radiating from her. With her black hair splayed on the pillow, she looked like a princess in a fairy tale. Her purple-blue eyes shone like rare jewels.

"You were very sweet to bring our meal in here, but to be honest, I'm not hungry. Don't you know I'm about to have the experience I've been waiting for all my life with my husband? Come to bed."

His lungs froze. "But your doctor sai—"

"Luckey, he was just teasing you."

"What?"

Her smile lit up his world. "The whole wing of the hospital knew about our wedding ceremony. I guess it's a man thing for him to give you a hard time." She sat up against the headboard. The sight of her bare arms and shoulders let him know she hadn't put on a nightgown. He could hardly swallow.

"When he asked me if I'd thought about protection, I told him I wanted a baby right away. He said I'd better check with you first. I have to tell you I'm hoping I'm pregnant by May, when we take our long honeymoon to the Grand Canyon with the horses. But if I'm not, we'll just keep trying, because from what I understand, that's the best part. I hope you won't be too shocked when I tell you I've never been to bed with a man before."

He blinked. "You're serious."

"Very. If that frightens you, I'm sorry, but I promise to be a good student."

Luckey couldn't take any more and headed for the bathroom. He showered in record time and hitched a towel around his hips before joining his new wife, who was absolutely the most amazing, astounding, surprising, luscious female he'd ever known.

Once under the covers, he came close to going up in smoke as she welcomed him into her arms. He forgot the world as they began to give each other the kind of divine pleasure that was beyond description. Luckey felt sorry for every man who would never

know what it was like to have a loving, giving, pas-
sionate wife like Ally.

"Sweetheart…you're so beautiful, it hurts."

"I feel that same pain just thinking about you.
Don't stop loving me. Don't ever stop."

"Never, Ally. Never."

They made love until afternoon, and then stopped
long enough to eat before beginning the whole process of loving each other all over again. Late the next
morning Luckey woke first and watched her sleep.
One arm lay folded against his chest, with her face
resting on his shoulder.

Since joining her in bed, he'd forgotten she'd just
come out of the hospital. He hoped to heaven their
hungry lovemaking hadn't done anything to set her
back. Luckey traced the line of the mouth that had
sent him into ecstasy with every touch. His index
finger found the little cut, which was almost healed.

For the first time, the sight he'd had of Martin
knocking her against the wall replayed in his mind.
He moaned in pain and gathered her in his arms,
bringing her awake.

"Darling?" she murmured.

"Forgive me. I love you so much, I'm depriving
you of sleep."

"I was only pretending. For the last half hour I've
been lying here wondering if you'd think I was terrible to kiss you awake."

He kissed both her eyelids. "Let's clear something
up right now. You never need permission to show me
your love."

"That's good, because I'm out of control and always will be. You have that effect on me."

Luckey pulled her on top of him. "I've been wondering what we should call our child if it's a boy."

"I'm way ahead of you, even if it's a girl."

A chuckle escaped. "I knew it. Give me a clue."

"The boy's first initial will be a *D*."

Luckey's chuckle turned into full-bodied laughter that shook the bed. "And the girl's?"

"A *D*, too."

He kissed her throat. "You really were obsessed with the Lone Ranger when you were little."

"Yup. I knew when I grew up I wanted my first boy to be Daniel, named for his older brother, who was killed."

"That means if we have a girl, we're calling her Danielle."

Ally looked down at him. "Do you mind? I'd like to keep it all in the family."

"How could I possibly mind that my wife has been in love with the masked man forever?"

"Oh, good. Now that I've married my own Texas Ranger hero, everything's going to be perfect!"

"What if we have a second child?" he teased, so crazily in love with his wife he never wanted to move from this spot.

"We could go with Reid, their last name, or…"

"Or what? I put my foot down at calling one of our children *Kemo Sabe*."

"How about we give that name to our toy horse?"

He cupped her face. "What toy horse?"

"The one I want us to buy for Persey and Silver. It'll make them feel like a family, too. Did you see how cute Comet was with Daken?"

Yes. He saw how cute. He saw how cute his wife was with Jeremy's horses. He saw how cute she'd be with children of her own. *Their* own. Life couldn't get better than this.

* * * * *

Keep reading for a sneak peek of
SUNRISE CROSSING,
the latest captivating novel in the acclaimed
RANSOM CANYON *series by*
New York Times *bestselling author*
Jodi Thomas!

CHAPTER ONE

Flight

January 2012
LAX

VICTORIA VILANIE CURLED into a ball, trying to make herself small, trying to disappear. Her black hair spread around her like a cape but couldn't protect her.

All the sounds in the airport were like drums playing in a jungle full of predators. Carts with clicking wheels rolling on pitted tiles. People shuffling and shouting and complaining. Electronic voices rattling off numbers and destinations. Babies crying. Phones ringing. Winter's late storm pounding on walls of glass.

Victoria, Tori to her few friends, might not be making a sound, but she was screaming inside.

Tears dripped off her face, and she didn't bother to wipe them away. The noise closed in around her, making her feel so lonely in the crowd of strangers.

She was twenty-four, and everyone said she was a

gifted artist. Money poured in so fast it had become almost meaningless, only a number that brought no joy. But tonight all she wanted was silence, peace, a world where she could hide out.

She scrubbed her eyes on her sleeve and felt a hand touch her shoulder like it were a bird, feather-light, landing there.

Tori turned and recognized a woman she'd seen once before. The tall blonde in her midthirties owned one of the best galleries in Dallas. Who could forget Parker Lacey's green eyes? She was a woman who had it all and knew how to handle her life. A born general who must manage her life as easily as she managed her business.

"Are you all right, Tori?" Parker asked.

Tori could say nothing but the truth. "I'm living the wrong life."

Then, the strangest thing happened. The lady with green eyes hugged her and Tori knew, for the first time in years, that someone had heard her, really heard her.

CHAPTER TWO

The stone-blue days of winter

February
Dallas, Texas

PARKER LACEY SAT perfectly straight on the side of her hospital bed. Her short, sunny-blond hair combed, her makeup in place and her logical mind in control of all emotions, as always.

She'd ignored the pain in her knee, the throbbing in her leg, for months. She ignored it now.

She'd been poked and examined all day, and now all that remained before the curtain fell on her life was for some doctor she barely knew to tell her just how long she had left to live. A month. Six months. If she was lucky, a year?

Her mother had died when Parker was ten. Breast cancer at thirty-one. Her father died eight years later. Lung cancer at thirty-nine. Neither parent had made it to their fortieth birthday.

Longevity simply didn't run in Parker's family. She'd known it and worried about dying all her adult life, and at thirty-seven, she realized her number would come up soon. Only she'd been smarter than all her ancestors. She would leave no offspring. There would be no next generation of Laceys. She was the last in her family.

There were also no lovers, or close friends, she thought. Her funeral would be small.

The beep of her cell phone interrupted her morbid thoughts.

"Hello, Parker speaking," she said.

"I'm in!" came a soft voice. "I followed the map. It was just a few miles from where the bus stopped. The house is perfect, and your housekeeper delivered more groceries than I'll be able to eat in a year. And, Parker, you were right. This isolated place will be heaven."

Parker forgot her problems. She could worry about dying later. Right now, she had to help one of her artists. "Tori, are you sure you weren't followed?"

"Yes. I did it just the way you suggested. Kept my head down. Dressed like a boy. Switched buses twice. One bus driver even told me to 'Hurry along, kid.'"

"Good. No one will probably connect me with you and no one knows I own a place in Crossroads. Stay there. You'll be safe. You'll have time to relax and think."

"They'll question you when they realize I've vanished," Tori said. "My stepfather won't just let me disappear. I'm worth too much money to him."

Parker laughed, trying to sound reassuring. "Of course, people will ask how well we know one another. I'll say I'm proud to show your work in my gallery and that we've only met a few times at gallery openings." Both facts were true. "Besides, it's no crime to vanish, Tori. You are an adult."

Victoria Vilanie was silent on the other end. She'd told Parker that she'd been on a manic roller coaster for months. The ride had left her fragile, almost shattered. Since she'd been thirteen and been "discovered" by the art community, her stepfather had quit his job and become her handler.

"Tori," Parker whispered into the phone. "You're not the tiger in a circus. You'll be fine. You can stand on your own. There are professionals who will help you handle your career without trying to run your life."

"I know. It's just a little frightening."

"It's all right, Tori. You're safe. You don't have to face the reporters. You don't have to answer any questions." Parker hesitated. "I'll come if you need me."

"I'd like that."

No one would ever believe that Parker would stick her neck out so far to help a woman she barely knew. Maybe she and Tori had each recognized a fellow loner, or maybe it was just time in her life that she did something different, something kind.

"No matter what happens," Tori whispered, "I want to thank you. You've saved my life. I think if I'd had to go another week, I might have shattered into a million pieces."

Parker wanted to say that she doubted it was that serious, but she wasn't sure the little artist wasn't right. "Stay safe. Don't tell the couple who take care of the house anything. You're just visiting, remember? Have them pick up anything you need from town. You'll find art supplies in the attic room if you want to paint."

"Found the supplies already, but I think I just want to walk around your land and think about my life. You're right. It's time I started taking my life back."

"I'll be there as soon as I can." Parker had read every mystery she could find since she was eight. If Tori wanted to disappear, Parker should be able to figure out how to make it happen. After all, how hard could it be?

The hospital door opened.

Parker clicked off the disposable phone she'd bought at the airport a few weeks ago when she and Tori talked about how to make Tori vanish.

"Miss Parker?" A young doctor poked his head into her room. He didn't look old enough to be out of college, much less med school, but this was a teaching hospital, one of the best in the country. "I'm Dr. Brown."

"It's Miss Lacey. My first name is Parker," she said as she pushed the phone beneath her covers. Hiding it like she was hiding the gifted artist.

The kid of a doctor moved into the room. "You any kin to Quanah Parker? We get a few people in here every year descended from the great Comanche chief."

She knew what the doctor was trying to do. Establish rapport before he gave her the bad news, so she played along. "That depends. How old was he when he died?"

The doctor shrugged. "I'm not much of a history buff, but my folks stopped at every historical roadside marker in Texas and Oklahoma when I was growing up. I think the great warrior was old when he died, real old. Had six wives, I heard, when he passed peacefully in his sleep on his ranch near a town that bears his name."

"If he lived a long life, I'm probably not kin to him. And to my knowledge, I have no Native American blood, and no living relatives." By the time she'd been old enough to ask, no one around remembered why she was named Parker and she had little interest in exploring a family tree with such short branches.

"I'm so sorry." Then he grinned. "I could give you a couple of my sisters. Ever since I got out of med school they think I'm their private *dial a doc*. They even call me to ask if TV shows get it right."

"No thanks, keep your sisters." She tried to smile.

"There are times when it's good to have family around." He said, "Would you like me to call someone for you? A close friend, maybe?"

She glanced up and read all she needed to know in the young man's eyes. She was dying. He looked terrible just giving her the news. Maybe this was the first time he'd ever had to tell anyone that their days were numbered.

"How long do I have to hang around here?"

The doc checked her chart and didn't meet her gaze as he said, "An hour, maybe two. When you come back, we'll make you as comfortable here as we can but you'll need—"

She didn't give him time to list what she knew came next. She'd watched her only cousin go through bone cancer when they were in high school. First, there would be surgery on her leg. Then they wouldn't get it all and she'd have chemo. Round after round until her hair and spirit disappeared. No, she wouldn't do that. She'd take the end head-on.

The doctor broke into her thoughts. "We can give you shots in that left knee. It'll make the pain less until—"

"Okay, I'll come back when I need it," she said not wanting to give him time to talk about how she might lose her leg or her life. If she let him say the word *cancer*, she feared she might start screaming and never stop.

She knew she limped when she was tired and her knee sometimes buckled on her. Her back already hurt, and her whole left leg felt weak sometimes. The cancer must be spreading; she'd known it was there for months, but she'd kept putting off getting a checkup. Now, she knew it would only get worse. More pain. More drugs, until it finally traveled to her brain. Maybe the doctor didn't want her to hang around and suffer? Maybe the shots would knock her out. She'd feel nothing until the very end. She'd just wait for death like her cousin had. She'd visited him every day. Watching him grow weaker, watching the staff grow sadder.

Hanging around had never been her way, and it wouldn't be now.

A nurse in scrubs that were two sizes too small

rushed into the room and whispered, loud enough for Parker to hear, "We've got an emergency, Doctor. Three ambulances are bringing injured in from a bad wreck. Pileup on I-35. Can you break away to help?"

The doctor flipped the chart closed. "No problem. We're finished here." He nodded to Parker. "We'll have time to talk later, Miss Parker. You've got a few options."

She nodded back, not wanting to hear the details, anyway. What did it matter? He didn't have to say the word *cancer* for her to know what was wrong.

He was gone in a blink.

The nurse's face molded into a caring mask. "What can I do to make you more comfortable? You don't need to worry, dear, I've helped a great many people go through this.

"You can hand me my clothes," Parker said as she slid off the bed. "Then you can help me leave." She was used to giving orders. She'd been doing it since she'd opened her art gallery fifteen years ago. She'd been twenty-two and thought she had forever to live.

"Oh, but..." The nurse's eyes widened as if she were a hen and one of her chickens was escaping the coop.

"No buts. I have to leave now." Parker raised her eyebrow silently, daring the nurse to question her.

Parker stripped off the hospital gown and climbed into the tailored suit she'd arrived in before dawn. The teal silk blouse and cream-colored jacket of polished wool felt wonderful against her skin compared to the rough cotton gown. Like a chameleon changing color, she shifted from patient to tall, in-control businesswoman.

The nurse began to panic again. "Is someone picking you up? Were you discharged? Has the paperwork already been completed?"

"No to the first question. I drove myself here and I'll drive myself away. And yes, I was discharged." Parker tossed her things into the huge Coach bag she'd brought in. If her days were now limited, she wanted to make every one count. "I have to do something very important. I've no time to mess with paperwork. Mail the forms to me."

Parker walked out while the nurse went for a wheelchair. Her mind checked off the things she had to do as her high heels clicked against the hallway tiles. It would take a week to get her office in order. She wanted the gallery to run smoothly while she was gone.

She planned to help a friend, see the colors of life and have an adventure. Then, when she passed, she would have lived, if only for a few months.

Climbing into her special edition Jaguar, she gunned the engine. She didn't plan to heed any speed-limit signs. *Caution* was no longer in her vocabulary.

The ache in her leg whispered through her body when she bent her knee, but Parker ignored it. No one had told her what to do since she entered college and no one, not even Dr. Brown, would set rules now.

REQUEST YOUR FREE BOOKS!
2 FREE NOVELS PLUS 2 FREE GIFTS!

H HARLEQUIN®

~Western ~Romance

ROMANCE THE ALL-AMERICAN WAY!

YES! Please send me 2 FREE Harlequin® Western Romance novels and my 2 FREE gifts (gifts are worth about $10). After receiving them, if I don't wish to receive any more books, I can return the shipping statement marked "cancel." If I don't cancel, I will receive 4 brand-new novels every month and be billed just $4.74 per book in the U.S. or $5.49 per book in Canada. That's a savings of at least 12% off the cover price! It's quite a bargain! Shipping and handling is just 50¢ per book in the U.S. and 75¢ per book in Canada.* I understand that accepting the 2 free books and gifts places me under no obligation to buy anything. I can always return a shipment and cancel at any time. Even if I never buy another book, the two free books and gifts are mine to keep forever.

154/354 HDN GJ5V

Name _____ (PLEASE PRINT) _____

Address _____ Apt. # _____

City _____ State/Prov. _____ Zip/Postal Code _____

Signature (if under 18, a parent or guardian must sign) _____

Mail to the **Reader Service:**
IN U.S.A.: P.O. Box 1867, Buffalo, NY 14240-1867
IN CANADA: P.O. Box 609, Fort Erie, Ontario L2A 5X3

Want to try two free books from another line?
Call 1-800-873-8635 or visit www.ReaderService.com.

* Terms and prices subject to change without notice. Prices do not include applicable taxes. Sales tax applicable in N.Y. Canadian residents will be charged applicable taxes. Offer not valid in Quebec. This offer is limited to one order per household. Not valid for current subscribers to Harlequin Western Romance books. All orders subject to credit approval. Credit or debit balances in a customer's account(s) may be offset by any other outstanding balance owed by or to the customer. Please allow 4 to 6 weeks for delivery. Offer available while quantities last.

Your Privacy—The Reader Service is committed to protecting your privacy. Our Privacy Policy is available online at www.ReaderService.com or upon request from the Reader Service.

We make a portion of our mailing list available to reputable third parties that offer products we believe may interest you. If you prefer that we not exchange your name with third parties, or if you wish to clarify or modify your communication preferences, please visit us at www.ReaderService.com/consumerschoice or write to us at Reader Service Preference Service, P.O. Box 9062, Buffalo, NY 14240-9062. Include your complete name and address.

HWR16

SPECIAL EXCERPT FROM

Ⓗ HARLEQUIN®

𝒲estern ℛomance

*Danny Leigh and Clover Van Camp have very different
ideas about how to revitalize Angel Crossing, Arizona.
But this isn't the first time the two of them have
tangled…*

*Read on for a preview of
THE BULL RIDER'S REDEMPTION,
the next book in Heidi Hormel's miniseries
ANGEL CROSSING, ARIZONA.*

"Clover?"

She turned and smiled, her perpetually red lips looking
as lush and kissable as they had been on that rodeo summer.
The one where Danny had won his buckle, lassoed a beauty
queen and lost his virginity.

"Hello, Danny," she said, a light drawl in her voice. "I
heard you were mayor of Angel Crossing. Congratulations."
She smiled again.

"Why did you buy those properties out from under
me?" he asked.

"Good investment." She turned back to the paperwork.

Danny wouldn't be dismissed. He wanted Angel
Crossing to thrive and he had plans for those properties.
He didn't want any of that to be ruined. Crossing his arms
over his chest, he stared at her…hat—not her jean-clad
rear and long legs.

Slowly, deliberately, she put down the pen and took the
papers before facing him. "What did you need, Danny?"

"I would like to know your plans for the properties, strictly as an official of the town."

"I don't think so." She looked him in the eye, nearly his height in her impractical pink cowgirl boots, matched to her cowgirl shirt. She looked the same, yet different. A woman grown into and comfortable with her blue-blood nose and creamy Southern-belle skin.

"There must be some reason you won't share your plans."

"It's business, Danny. That's all. It was nice to see you." She turned from him before he could say anything else and he watched her walk away. A beautiful sight, as it always had been. Tall, curvier than she'd been at eighteen and proud.

Now, though, what she was up to was important to him. To Angel Crossing, too. If she wouldn't tell him what she was up to, he'd find out on his own. He wasn't the big dumb cowboy who was led around by his gonads anymore. He was a responsible adult who had a town to look after…

Don't miss
THE BULL RIDER'S REDEMPTION
by Heidi Hormel, available October 2016 wherever
Harlequin® Western Romance®
books and ebooks are sold.

www.Harlequin.com